ABSOLUTION is the third boo
Series and completes the trilc
are **BODY IN THE WOOD** and
both are available to purchase as paperbacks on
Amazon or to download from the Kindle Store.

PROLOGUE

From the minute that I had received the call, I knew that time was not on my side. I run straight past the nurse and into the room, the scent of the hospital-grade disinfectant, was now sadly all too familiar.

"I'm here..." I say softly to her, whilst I try to grab hold of one of her hands to provide comfort. I struggle in my task, as they are tucked in tightly under the crisp white sheets. Once freed, I wrap my fingers into hers. I then realise that they are unusually cool. In my rush to get to her, I hadn't noticed that the matron had followed me into the room. She comes over to the side of the bed where I am stood, and placing her hand gently on my shoulder she says "I'm so sorry darling, they should have said... she's already gone."

Shelley

I look out across the Normandy landscape, observing the corn stalks swaying in the breeze, and the dazzling sun looking like a yellow jewel against the bright blue sky. Josephine is in the swimming pool, playing with the girls. I can hear both Heidi and Maggie squealing with delight, clearly having fun as they splash their Nana Jo Jo.

"Oh John, I wish we could stay here forever. This was such a good idea. It's just what we needed, and I am so glad that she came. Look at her. The girls love her, I love her. I didn't realise it, but she really is my missing piece."

John

It was shortly after that day, that I decided that we all needed a break. After what I had learnt, I had become very wary of my new mother-in-law, and I was pretty confident that she was a serial killer. Joseph, I was sure had not been her only victim, and in normal circumstances, of course, I would have arrested her. She would have been charged, and rightly locked up. However, this was anything but normal. This was family.

For years I had watched my wife struggle. Struggle with who she was, and where she had come from. She had always thought that she wasn't good enough. Truth be told, she was more than good enough. She was perfect. Clever, witty, intelligent. She was a people person, and everyone warmed to her. She always put them at ease…. Well, she definitely did now, now that they knew that she wasn't a murderer… Her mother, however, she was a different matter altogether. She _was_ a convicted killer.

Josephine

I couldn't believe that they had invited me to go with them. After everything that had happened, John felt it would be a good idea to get away from it all. I had spoken to my probation officer; Mary. A lovely lady, super unorganised, even though she still seemed to know her stuff. Anyway, she had confirmed that I could travel outside of the UK, and I would not be in breach of any of my conditions.

So, here we are in their neighbour's Gite. From what I can gather, it's not even cost us a penny. A gift apparently. Their neighbour, Janice or Jackie, or whatever her name is, she feels at fault for having spoken to the police. The silly woman, she thinks that she was responsible for getting Shelley convicted…. Utter nonsense, as only I am truly responsible, and although Shelley says that it is water under the bridge… I still feel guilty.

The Gite is like no other cottage that I have ever stayed in. There's a pool, sauna, the bubbly outside bath thingy that everyone raves about, and it's all located within the middle of the sprawling French countryside. Considering where I thought I would be a couple of months ago, it really does feel like I have died and gone to heaven! There is the main house and an annex. I'm in the annex of course, and I don't mind that one bit. It is good for them and me, to still have our own space. This whole being a mum and having a family, as well as being a grandma, is still something that I am adjusting to. Not that I'm complaining; it's the best job that I've ever had.

DS Rachel Cooper

After John's call, I was convinced that he knew something. I was at the time, knee-deep in a historical case that concerned a missing child. I had tried calling him back, but he didn't pick up. Anyway, on this old case, but new to me; my victim had gone to the playground to meet her friends, but she had never made it. The original investigation had initially suspected the parents and when that led nowhere, the then next-door neighbour, but again there was no evidence to suggest that he was involved. Rosie was her name, and every witness statement that I had read gave me the opinion that she was a happy little girl. She had no need to run away, and there was absolutely no suggestion that she had. Therefore, having reviewed the whole case-file, I came to the same conclusion as the original Senior Investigating Officer…. It had to be foul play… Anyway, Kevin (DI Smart) wanted a result on this one, and I knew he'd not thank me if I got sidetracked again with Josephine Gilling. If John had got something to say, I'm sure he would share it. I have heard on the grapevine for now that he's on holiday, having some well-deserved family time. I'll just have to catch up with him when he is back.

John

"So, you really want to stay here, do you?" I ask Shelley this as we are sat on the patio, having just finished our dinner. Josephine has already taken the girls inside for a bath. She really has stepped up to the plate, as far as grandmother duties are concerned. Shelley swills her white wine around her glass and contemplates my question.

"Well… Could we? Maybe not forever, as I would miss Mum and Dad too much… but we could take some time out? Have some proper family time? No one knows us here. No one knows what happened."

"Are you sure? Long-term in France?"

"Yes, just think about it… We could rent out our house, and Mum could rent out her flat. I'm sure Jeanette would do us a deal… she still feels responsible, you know…"

"Well... I don't know why she does... It wasn't her who skipped off on her holidays, and left you to rot in a prison cell!"

I can tell that I have touched a nerve. Shelley immediately snaps her head around exorcist style, and looks at me squarely in the eyes...

"What do you mean by that? She skipped nowhere, and I did not rot! She was in shock! She was ill, and she came back to save me as soon as she felt better. She handed herself in, John!"

"Yes, yes, I know." Trying to calm the conversation with my lowered tone...

"Look, I thought you liked her. I thought that's why you invited her here. She's my mum, John! I'm part of her..."

I knew I shouldn't have said anything, but I'm still angry that I could have lost Shelley, and it would have been all of her fault. I know that Shelley is protective over her, so I really should have known better than to say anything. It was that second glass of wine that did it... It made my mouth run away with itself! I really should stick to beer.... I immediately apologise to Shelley, but I know that the damage has already been done, and she's got the hump...

"Sorry, darling. I do like her. I like how good she is for you... Anyway, if you're serious about all of this and you really want this change of scene... I'll even think about a career break..."

I know that she isn't even listening to me anymore, as she doesn't acknowledge what I have just said...

"Right! I'm going to go and help Mum." And with that, she's gone. Yep! I've annoyed her... I honestly don't think that I'll ever be able to share the suspicions that I have over her mother... Well, not without losing her. What is it they say about blood being thicker than water?!

Josephine

They sat me down at the table, and I really thought that I had done something wrong. Both of them were so serious looking. Anyway, it turns out that they are considering relocating to France, on a more permanent basis. John is thinking about taking a sabbatical, and Shelley has decided to put her return to the University on hold. To say that I was disappointed, would have been an understatement. I had only just found her, found them, and now they wanted to stay here permanently. Apparently, they had spoken to Jeanette, and she was happy to give them the Gite on a long-term let. There was space in the local school for the girls, and both Shelley and John had agreed that it would probably be one of the best experiences, that they could ever offer them. They would be immersed in the culture and learn French. "...they are such sponges Mum, they'll be bilingual..."

"Yes, it all sounds wonderful…" I say, trying to be positive, and hide the fact that I felt that the proverbial rug, had just been pulled out from beneath me…. I didn't want to lose my family, not again.

I'm not really listening, as I'm upset by the news… I thought she had wanted me in her life… Anyway, Shelley clearly not noticing the disappointment in my face, she carries on telling me about their plans… "So, as we said, John is going to apply for a career break… and we can rent out our house… and sooner or later, I'll be getting some sort of compensation from the government, plus if we really do run out of money, we can just pick plums!" I can hear the excitement in her voice…

"So, Mum, what do you think?" I drag myself out of my own gloomy thoughts, and I try again to sound upbeat.
"Well, yes, it's a lovely idea…"
"You really think so?"

"Although.... are you sure you've really thought this all through? What about the University? Should you really delay returning? .... You said yourself, catching up even now would be difficult?"

"Oh, Mum it's fine. I will go back... but I need this time. We all do. I thought you would have jumped at it."

"Jumped at losing you again? Why? Why would I want you, John, and the girls over here, whilst I'm over there?"

"Oh, Mum, don't be daft! We meant all of us. You could speak to Imogen, and you could rent out your flat? You could even help me pick the plums!"

"You and your bleeding plums!! Are you serious? You want me too?"

"Yes, Mum! John and I have spoken about it, and there is no way that we would leave you at home alone. John has already said, that if you don't want to come, or probation have a problem with it, then it is a non-starter!"

John is nodding his head in agreement, and I realise that my eyes have started to leak, I can feel tears of joy begin to trail down my face...

"Really? You honestly want me too?"

"Yes, Mum! So, what do you say?" I didn't even think about it, not even for a second, as excitedly I reply...

"I say yes!!"

Shelley

John is at his sabbatical leaving drinks, AKA any old excuse for a booze-up…. We came home for a fortnight to get things organised, and I'm busy packing up all of our personal stuff into boxes. Mum is doing the same. She's going to rent her place out furnished, but any personal bits that she has, she is bringing them here for me to squeeze into our already full loft. To help with this process, I have also got a skip on the driveway. It is so therapeutic chucking everything away. Broken toys, old books, CD's, videos… We just don't need them anymore. So long as we have got the internet; we can listen, watch or read whatever we like… I have never been so ruthless, but after the time I have had, I have come to realise that possessions mean nothing, it's all about the memories.

The doorbell rings… It is Mum. Not Josephine, but Mum, Mum. She has been wonderful throughout all of this. For ages I had felt so guilty about running off to the French countryside, and when I told her of my plan to relocate permanently, she was so supportive. No trying to sway me… straight away she replied "Darling, I think that is just what you need… I think it's a great idea…"

Anyway, today I've invited her over for lunch, just me and her.

Josephine

I had my heart in my mouth when Mary, my probation officer, had called me back. I had asked her at the beginning of the week whether it might be a possibility. When she finally called me, it was actually good news. She advised that she had looked into it, and there would be no problems with my plan of a longer-term relocation. I was ecstatic... She said so long as I kept in touch, she would happily manage me remotely ... She even joked saying that we could have our 1-2-1's by the pool! I still can't believe how lenient they have been with me. Sometimes I think that they have forgotten about what I actually did. Imogen too, she immediately agreed to my sabbatical. She even recommended the letting agent that her nephew had used. New Beginnings; .... I have an agent from there coming around later to assess the flat, take some pictures and to get it advertised. I still can't believe how easy this has all been. I keep expecting something to go wrong...

DS Rachel Cooper

I've had a busy week trawling through statement after statement. I'm still trying to piece together Rosie's final movements. Sometimes I wonder why I do this to myself, and why I am even in Cold Cases? Why did I not stick with the jobs where the witnesses were still alive and there is even a chance of some CCTV? I had been getting very disheartened of late, but then I stop myself, and I think about poor Rosie's parents... They had been looking for their little girl for years. I had to keep focused, and I really hoped that I would be the one to finally find her.

Anyway, I'm almost done for the day, when I spot a name that I recognise; it is Eric Frost. Apparently, he had been spoken to at the time of her disappearance. He had been doing some work at a neighbouring property. The original Investigative Team had taken a witness statement, but had never considered him as a suspect. As I had no one else, I decided to start with him. However not now, not tonight…. I was shattered so I was off to the Green Bottle for a well-deserved Pinot and an unwind.

John

"I'm going to miss this place… I still remember coming here to wet the girls' heads. It only seems like yesterday… I can't believe how quickly that the years have gone by…"

"I know, Mate. Both of mine are at university now… costing me a flipping fortune… I won't be retiring anytime soon… and I'm 55 next month too!"

"Ah, you'd miss it!"

"I'm not sure that I would to be honest. This is a young man's game."

I'm mid-conversation, and busy chewing the cud when I look round and I see her; it's Rachel.

She immediately makes eye contact with me, and makes her way over to our table.

"Oh, Hi John, how fortuitous… I've been meaning to catch up with you. I never managed to get to the bottom as to why you called me that time?"

I immediately feel uneasy…

"Called you?" *I know exactly what she is talking about, and I had hoped that she would have forgotten!*

"Yes, you seemed very interested in my cold cases. I just wondered what had piqued your interest?"

"Ah, now I remember, sorry Rachel. It was nothing."

"Really? Are you sure?" *I say nothing...*

"Anyway, what are you doing here then? Who's leaving do is it this time?"

"Well, mine actually. It's not a permanent thing, just a sabbatical. I think we all need a break. So, we have decided to take some time out and we are going to live in France for a bit."

"Ah, that will be nice for Shelley. Although, isn't she going to miss her mum though? Seeing as she has only just got to meet her?"

"No. Actually... she's coming too!"

"Are you sure she will be allowed? Probation are quite prescriptive as to what you can and cannot do."

"It's not a problem apparently... We've checked, and they have already OK'd it."

"Really?!"

I can tell in her voice that she is shocked. To be honest, I was too when I found out. However, I really wouldn't have felt comfortable leaving her behind in the UK, unsupervised. I know that I haven't got any cast-iron proof, but I'm pretty sure that all is not as it seems when it comes to my mother-in-law.

"Yes, that's right, so long as she keeps in touch…"
"They didn't get her mixed up with a shoplifter, did they? They do know that she is a convicted killer?" *She says this rather aggressively…*
"Calm down Rachel!" *A little taken aback at her obvious anger.*
"Sorry John! It must be the wine!"
"No problem…" *having noticed that she has immediately gone red, clearly embarrassed by her ferocious outburst …*

"I'm exactly the same on the vino, hence me sticking to pints."

"Anyway…" *she says after composing herself…* "When are you off?"

"Next week. We have just got a few things to tie up… Both us and Josephine are going to rent out our places…. and then we're away."

"Ok, then…"

With that, she has left us to it and we resume chatting….

"Blimey! What was all that about? Is she still trying to pin those murders onto Shelley's mum?"

"Yup, and there is no sign of her giving up!"

"Another pint, Mate?"

"Ah go on then."

Ben goes up to the bar and I'm left at the table. I feel a little deflated after seeing Rachel. I know I should be excited about the break, but I can't help but feel that I'm letting myself, the Force and those victims down.

DS Rachel Cooper

So, I see John in the pub. I may have slightly embarrassed myself as I was somewhat overzealous, but I finally got to ask him about the call. He played it down and said it was nothing, but I know he knows something and get this.... They are running away!

Josephine

I have not stopped this past week, and I have done that many trips to the dump that I have lost count.... It really is a case of out with the old. I have packed up my "keep" pile, and I've just arrived at Shelley and John's.
"Hi, Mum!" Shelley shouts this from the front door...
"Do you need a hand bringing that in?"
"Oh no, it's fine. It's only two boxes. I didn't realise how little I had, that was actually important to me."
"Well, you've done better than me... I've skipped most of our stuff, and the loft; it is still packed to the rafters... It is a good job really that you haven't got much, I wouldn't know where to put it all!"
I walk past her carrying one of my boxes, and I pop it down just inside..."
"Did John tell you? One of his mates from work is going to rent the house?"
"No... Oh, that's wonderful news ..."

"Well, not really for him...he has just split from his wife. He's got two kiddies too... So, he will be having them every other week... It's not for the full market value, but at least we know him."

I've not been quite so lucky with renting out my flat. It's advertised, but no viewings as yet. Hopefully soon...

"Oh yes... Mum, before I forget, John wanted me to give you this."

"What is it?" I say looking at the box.

"What does it look like? It's a new phone. It's all set up apparently and ready to go..."

There was nothing wrong with my old one, so I was a little confused, but I thanked her anyway...

"Say thanks to John for me."

"Yep, will do... Right then Mum, shall we have a cuppa? And then we can get on with playing Tetris. I've already put up your shoebox full of all your old pics."

DS Rachel Cooper

Apparently, they have all gone off to France. I don't begrudge John or Shelley, but it does seem a bit of a liberty that she has gone too… Off again on her holidays. The law really is an ass. They (MP's that is), always say that there will be harsher sentences for carrying knives, but we all know that they will say anything just to get elected. It never bloody happens! No wonder so many kids are killing kids! I still can't get over the fact that she got a bloody suspended sentence. It's all so wrong!

Kev has already told me that I need to focus on the job at hand, and I really don't want to let him down. I pull out the Rosie Flood case-file, and I start going through all of the statements again... I'm naturally drawn to the one from Eric Frost. He states that he was doing some work next door to the victim's address, and that he had noticed the happy young six-year-old. He said how friendly she was, and that she had waved at him several times on her way past. There was nothing more of significance in the statement, other than that he was with his wife at the time of the child's disappearance. He had apparently taken her out to do some shopping for her birthday. On reading this, I knew immediately who I needed to speak to... So, I had a chat with Kev, and he agreed that I should get a prison visit with the wife. She was currently at HMP Featherwater, serving a rather lengthy sentence for his murder. I made the calls and I got the paperwork signed. I was seeing her tomorrow. Best to strike whilst the iron is hot!

Josephine

I can't quite believe how quickly we have all settled in. We drove over as a convoy, down to Dover and then on to the ferry. I don't think I have ever been so excited. I still have a few concerns as my flat isn't yet rented out, but the agent called me this morning, and he let me know that he has got some interest, and hopefully some viewings would be arranged for this week.

I could get used to this slower pace of life, and I certainly love being here with Shelley and the girls. John seems to be a little distracted of late, but maybe it is the worry of not being employed. It must be really hard leaving something like policing behind. It is meant to be in your blood.

DS Rachel Cooper

Kelly Frost was immediately recognisable from her custody image that we still had on file, and luckily for her, she appeared not have aged. She was quite a petite woman, with long hair. In fact, when I was sat with her in the flesh, I had noticed that she had an uncanny resemblance to Josephine Gilling. *(Maybe I was a little obsessed?!)*

Now, as the saying goes, once bitten, twice shy, so I had made sure that I was extra careful at this prison visit. I didn't dare mention that I thought that she might be innocent. Although that was the first thing that had come out of her mouth!
"You know, I didn't do it... I don't know what your lot do well, but it's not punishing those who need it. Do you know that 50% of us in here are innocent, and you do absolutely nothing about resolving it... Anyway, you

said you were here to talk about my husband? Well, he is dead in case you weren't sure!"

"Yes, I know... but it's actually concerning him when he was alive. Do you remember the Rosie Flood case?"

"I remember the name ..."

"It was the disappearance of that 6-year-old in 1986. She was meant to be meeting friends at the park but never made it..."

"Yes, I remember 1986 well. I'm sure the Bangles, 'Walk Like an Egyptian' was at number one for weeks... God, I loved that song!" *She starts humming the tune.*

"Ok... Umm, but do you remember the missing girl?"

"To be honest... yes I do. Her disappearance seemed to really spook Eric. He said that the police had spoken to him... and after that, I think is when we moved over to Essex. I'd not known him that long but he was adamant, saying the area just wasn't safe anymore.... In fact, at the time I had been pleased that he was looking out for my little girl... Little did I know back then what a bastard he really was!"

"I've got his statement here. It says here that he was out shopping with you for your birthday at the time of her going missing. Is that right?"

"I know I said that I remembered 1986 well, but you are asking me to remember back to thirty-four years ago."

"Yes, I know, but can you try?"

"To be honest, I can't remember, but I do know this. 1986 or not, Eric never took me shopping for my birthday. He was more of a last-minute bunch of chrysanthemums, kind of a man. Never from a florist neither, his shop of choice was the local petrol station. I don't really know why I married him. It was just after Jodie's Dad had died, I wanted security and he was there. A horrible man really. I don't regret his death for a minute. Do you know what he did to my daughter?"

"Yes, I know he was charged."

"Yes, and I failed her. I knew what he was like. I'll never forgive myself for what I let him do to her, but I was scared that I'd be left alone."

"Ok, sorry …" I am desperately trying to get a straight answer out of this woman, and it's proving to be hard work…

"So, are you saying that you weren't out shopping?"

"Yep…definitely. It's impossible…. Why the interest anyway? Why now?"

"Sorry, I thought I had explained. I work in Cold Cases, and Rosie's disappearance is being revisited."

"Ok, well if there is anything I can help with…. There is not much for me to do in here…. They won't even consider me for parole as I won't admit to it. Why the hell should I? I didn't do it. Sometimes I wished that I had, and then I would have been the one to have gotten Jodie her justice. It's so hard, even now talking to her. She says that she has forgiven me, and that she understands, but how can she. As a mother, you are meant to put your child first…."

"So, you have a relationship then?"

"Yes, she visits. She got in touch after my granddaughter was born."

"Oh! Congratulations!"

"Thank you. It's not a recent thing. She's a teenager now. Locked up in here, I missed out on everything. I'm none too keen on her partner neither…. He sounds just like Eric!"

"Sorry, can we go back to 1986? Where were you living before the move?"

"Cross Lane, although it's not there anymore. It got demolished years ago."

"Oh OK..." My face obviously showed my disappointment...

"You might want to try his old lockup by the marshes, if you think he was involved... Maybe he took her there?" She says this quite flippantly... but I take this intel very seriously. I have a lead and I already know what my next move is going to be.

Shelley

I never really realised just how important it was for me to have family. I don't mean my adoptive parents, or even John and the girls. I mean being able to look in the mirror and to know exactly who my eyes, my nose, and even my mouth came from. To know why I was left-handed and why I was so determined. Why I got sunburnt, and why Mum and Dad never did, and also why I laugh in the way that I do. Through finding my mum, I had finally been given all of those answers. I know that when I had first read the diary, I was so disgusted at my creation. I had been sickened that in my veins pumped his blood, but none of that seemed to matter anymore, not now that I had her, not now that I had my mum.

DS Rachel Cooper

DI Smart and I discussed the meeting that I had had with Kelly Frost. He had agreed with me that it was a fresh angle, and so he began sorting out the warrant for lockup, and getting a search team put together. I had carried on looking through the file, and I came across some old newspaper cuttings. One of them was of Rosie, she was at the local library with a couple of friends. She had joined up for the Readathon and the local press had covered it. I was sat at my desk, and looking at the grainy image when I saw her in the background of the shot. It was definitely her. A younger-looking Josephine Gilling. I really felt like she was haunting me. I knew that she was involved in all of this. Maybe not directly, but something definitely kept putting her onto my radar.

I still wanted to know why John had called me that day. Had she said something? Or had he seen something that didn't quite add up…. Or maybe it did? I knew I couldn't speak to Kev about it. I knew that he thought that I was a little fixated… Well, he hadn't said it in so many words, but I knew that was what was in his mind…. Also, I would never get a search warrant with just a hunch, well not with this. So, I did a Jo Gordon and I bent the rules. I made an appointment with her letting agent, and organised a viewing of her flat. I know that we had searched her address before, you know, when she had handed herself in, but I am not convinced that they did a proper job.

John

"Where's your mum, Shelley?"

"I don't know... she said that she had fancied a walk..."

"She's not taken her phone..." I'm trying to sound calm, but I am anything but! She has been spending more time in the village of late, and she has gotten to know a few of the locals. I'm pleased that she is integrating. We all are... The girls have made some friends, and they've even had a few playdates. Maggie was initially a little upset when she had found out that lapin was rabbit! She'd had Lapin a la Cocotte and positively raved about it, begging Shelley to make it, until that was... she found out that she'd actually eaten poor Flossie! Well, not the real Flossie... but you get the gist....

"Well ... She is allowed to go out, John! She's not in prison!"

"Yes, I know... I just get concerned.... She doesn't really know the area..."

"Who doesn't know the area?" Josephine says this, as she walks into the kitchen.

"Ah, there you are… John was getting worried, he thought that you'd gone AWOL…"

"No not AWOL… I just fancied a wander. I have found a wonderful woodland walk. You'll have to join me next time…"

"Yes, lovely Mum…Will do. I meant to say… I've asked the farmer about some fruit picking. Do you fancy doing some with me, Mum?"

"Go on then. It will be fun… Are you OK, John?"

"Yes fine. It's just, in future, please take your phone, OK? I like to know where you are…."

"It sounds to me like you are tracking me… "

"Oh, don't be daft, it's just important that you can call us if anything happens…"

"Nothing is going to happen…" She has clearly seen my serious face, so she then follows this up with… "OK, I promise… I'll take it in future."

"Thanks, Mum. He does worry. He's a copper to the core… John, you do need to chill out a bit, maybe you need to come with us and pick some plums!" She says this clearly trying to lighten the mood. Thankfully it works, as I instantly raise an eyebrow and a smile!

DS Rachel Cooper

I've got the day off so I am at the gym. I've not been there in absolute months. My head has been elsewhere so unfortunately, my body has suffered. That is the problem with me, I'm an all or nothing kind of a girl. Anyway, I looked in the full-length mirror this morning, and I was ashamed of what I saw.

I'm just on the treadmill, trying to prevent a full-on hyperventilation, when I see Stuart from work. I was on Team with him years back, when I had just started out as a probationer. He has been in the job for some twenty-odd years, and now he is in the Firearms Department. He comes towards me and I'm not exactly looking my best…. My face is berry-red and I'm trying my hardest to catch my breath!

"Hiya Rachel, long time…. I didn't know you came here?"

"Neither did I to be honest… First day back after months!" I mouth this at him as I'm trying to run and talk at the same time…

"I'll leave you to it … See you for a coffee later?"

"I can't Stu…" and by now, I've pressed pause so I can actually speak. "I'm viewing a flat in a bit…"

"I didn't know you were moving, I thought you had only bought last year?"

"I did… and I'm not really, I just like to see what's out there."

"Ah ok… talking about moving… I have just moved myself."

I'm still sweating and desperate to finish off my run, but he clearly wants to chat…. He is still hovering by my machine, so being polite, I say…

"Oh, lovely. Where did you buy? Still local?"

"Actually, I'm renting. Kate and I are on a trial separation…. I try to make my face look concerned… although, I could do without being an agony aunt today… He continues…

"She couldn't cope with the long hours, and me not helping enough with the kids, so... she has kicked me out!"

"Oh Stu, I'm so sorry to hear that. How are the kids?" I say really not caring either way...

"It's OK. To be honest they are quite excited. They now have two houses!"

"So where is it that you have rented?"

"My mate's place.... Him and his Mrs are off on a sabbatical to France. It's worked out quite well really.... It's fully furnished and they've done me a really good deal.... He is a brave bastard... He has even taken along the Mother-In-Law!"

"Oh really? Yes, he sounds it!" I say this with an air of excitement.

"Anyway, I've got to finish my run.... Stu, great to see you. Maybe I'll take you up on the coffee another day?"

"Yes great, that'll be lovely... well that's if you are in here again. It's my second home these days.... well third, if you count my new and old pad… of which I am still paying the mortgage on!!"

I laugh again and then I crank up the speed on the machine. I watch him as he wanders over to the weights area. He is a bit of a silver fox. Nice eye candy, if you know what I mean… He is also a really nice guy too. He was good to me when I first started. He helped me out with the paperwork, and in navigating around all of the systems. Which was unusual, as a lot of the old sweats just saw you as their pen. Once they have a probationer, their view is that they never have to write another statement, or make a bleeding cuppa ever again! Stu was different. Anyway, I have a feeling that I'll be seeing a lot more of him, especially knowing where he has just moved in to….

Josephine

It's really quite relaxing, hard work, yes... but definitely relaxing. You just pick and pack, pick and pack. I love the repetition of it.... I have even made some friends here, and I have never really done that.... Shelley seems to have given me the confidence that I have never had before. I clearly needed her, just as much as she had needed me. John is always saying that he wouldn't know how Shelley would cope again without me. A silly thing for him to say really, as I'm not going anywhere. As far as I'm concerned, this is me now. I have my family and I'll protect them forevermore, and that means my sticking around.

The agent, he called me again this morning, apparently, they have another viewing this afternoon. I wish they would call me with an actual let. I know I asked them to keep me in the loop, but all I really care about is that there is money coming in. I know I don't have a mortgage, but I was really hoping the rent would fund me out here. Plum picking is fun, but I can't see me doing it forever! Anyway, I'll keep my fingers crossed for today, and hopefully, when they next ring me, it will be because the contract is signed.

DS Rachel Cooper

I get to the red brick block just in the nick of time. The estate agent is stood outside, just by his logo'ed up Mini-Cooper. He is a tall and wiry looking ginger-haired chap, and he can't have been much older than eighteen. He is stood there in his grey waistcoated suit. They really do all look the same. You can always tell an estate agent a mile off!

"Hi, Rachel, is it?"

"Um.... Yes, sorry I'm a little late."

"No problem... been to the gym? I take it that you're local then?"

"Yes, to both, the gym and local..." God, this boy could be a detective. He is straight in with the questions.

"So, where are you at the moment?"

"Up on Wrens Square. Do you know it?"

"Yes, new builds, aren't they? They are lovely from what I have heard. So why are you looking to move?"

"Well, I'm not really…." I stop myself. I'd briefly got distracted by a text message that had come through on my watch, and I lost my train of thought!

"You were saying? You're not looking to move?" He looks at me quizzically.

"No, I am looking to move, I'm just not sure of where to move to at this stage."

"Ok, and if you don't mind me asking why are you?"

"Moving?"

"Yes"

"I've just split from my husband. He is a policeman and he is just never around…" Thank you, Stu, I think to myself, the perfect of cover stories…

"Well, I'm sorry to hear that. I hear that quite regularly in this job. It must be a tough role though. I always fancied it myself as a kid. Cops and robbers, fast cars and the like."

"Well yes, it's not too late you know, you could still join."

"Nah, I see you need a degree these days and the starting salary is just not worth it. I'm on an absolute mint flogging houses…."

"Ok. Right, shall we get in and see the place?"

"Yes lovely. It's on the top floor." He goes straight into his sales pitch… "So, being on the top, as a lone female you immediately have the security of not being on a ground level. We also have a key fob and intercom system, so no one can walk into the block without being let in. There is also CCTV which the Management Company monitor…"

"Oh lovely, great…" I try to sound interested…

We go into the porch, and then through the front door, and into the communal area. I then follow him up the flight of stairs that are just ahead of us. He carries on with his sell. "So, there's parking for two cars so if you did have any guests, they haven't got to hunt about for a space… Right, here we go. Both Chubb and Yale locks, for more peace of mind. In fact, the owner is a single female, and she was quite security conscious. All the windows have locks on them as you'll see."

"Actually, can I ask… why is she letting?"

"She's gone off to France, I think. Moved over with family."

"Oh, OK, and she's left her furniture?"

"Yes, it's let furnished."

"Oh ok… and is there further storage? A loft perhaps?"

"No not that I'm aware of. There are fitted wardrobes but nothing more than that."

"Is that a deal-breaker then? Have you a lot of stuff?"

"Um… no not really, I was just wondering where the owner might have stored all of her belongings. It's like a show home. Nothing personal anywhere."

"Yes, it's presented really well. You could just move in. Just pop a cushion here or picture up there, and you've made it your own."

"Sorry to go on, but do you know where they have stored their stuff?"

"Well, not that it has any bearing on you, if you do take it, but I think they said they were storing their personal belongings at their daughter's address. So, it's not anything you'll have to worry about..."

"Ah ok. Um... I'm not worried as such, (I think fast) but I looked at a place the other day and one of the rooms was locked, and when I asked why, the agent said it was full of the owner's stuff!"

"Well, as you can see that's not an issue here, being only one bedroom and one reception room, there are no others, bar the bathroom and kitchen and they are rather essential..."

"Ah yes," I say with a smile.

We walk around the pokey little flat, him pointing out this feature and that. I've totally lost interest. I was hoping to find a stash of her stuff that I could have trawled through, slow time. There was never any chance of me getting a warrant; DI Smart would never support it, so this had been the only way. I knew that she had a hand in his death, and maybe the Rosie Flood case was the key to unlocking the truth.

"Right then, what do you think, can you see yourself here?"

"Um…thanks for your time, but no. I've not really found what I'm looking for."

"Ok, no problem. Shall I keep you on my list? I can send you out some more potential properties?"

"Actually no, it's fine. I think I'll look elsewhere."

"Ok then, well… let me show you out. I've got another viewing at midday."

"Ok thank you, and do think about the police. It's a good career choice…" I said this having forgotten myself briefly, but it didn't matter… I no longer needed to keep up the pretence anyway.

Shelley

Mum called me today and it was just lovely to hear her voice. She had said that she was just checking in, and making sure that we were all ok. She and Dad had just come back from a week away in Cornwall. I do feel guilty for leaving them behind. Mum keeps telling me that she doesn't mind, but I know that she really misses the girls. We have tried FaceTime calls but the girls have such a short attention span, they either wander off, leaving Mum and Dad on the other end of the screen not knowing what is happening, or they just won't come over to the phone. I hate it as I know it must really upset Mum, when they say that they don't want to speak to her. John really erupted at them the last time that we tried it, and Heidi bless her, she was in tears. I really don't understand him at the moment. Ever since we got here, he has been on edge. He is even worse now, than he ever was when we were at home in the UK. Yes, I know that he was always risk assessing, or 'being prepared', as he called it. You know if we went into a restaurant with the girls, he would have immediately worked out our exit route; which was usually through the kitchen, and he would never ever allow us to sit in the window. Too much glass apparently. All of this planning was just in case there was a terrorist attack. "Why make yourself the target, Shell? Let someone else be the victim!"

Out here, nothing has really changed. He is permanently on his phone, and if I didn't know him any better, I would have thought that he had left a mistress behind in the UK. Well, it would certainly explain it…. He is constantly in a bad mood, and maybe the checking of his phone is him trying, but clearly failing at keeping her sweet!

DS Rachel Cooper

I'm up early, Kevin had arranged the warrant and search team for down at the Marshes for a 06:00 hours start. I drive down and I can already see a hive of activity. He is the Senior Investigating Officer on this one. I have just been doing the donkey work. It suits me, after all, we are all one team, and I know that he will share the credit if this pays off. Something Ma'am was sometimes reluctant to do. It was all so dependent on her mood. I suppose I should be a little grateful to her, as I wouldn't actually be here without her earlier assistance...
Anyway, they have located his old lockup. It's pretty much derelict, and it doesn't look like it's been touched since he last used it. Strange really, as it definitely has a commercial value to it. There is quite a lot of square footage.

It is my first time being involved in this type of investigation. You know, where you are looking for the body. I'm still relatively new to all of this, and from what I understand the success rates of actually discovering one, are still pretty low. They have been looking on the Saddleworth Moors for poor little Keith Bennett, one of Ian Brady's victims since the 1960's, and even with the scientific advances, and the use of drones and radar, they still haven't located him. I really do have my fingers crossed for this one. I am hoping that with a smaller search area that we will have more success.

Yesterday, I had attended Rosie's parents address, just to let them know of our intentions. The last thing I wanted was for them to find out through the press. We sadly can at times be a little sloppy, and if a copper or forensic examiner with a loosened tongue briefly forgets about confidentiality, and mentions what is happening at work to the wrong person. All of a sudden, the hope that the family has held on to for years, it is extinguished in a headline! It's funny isn't it, you would much rather think of your loved one being imprisoned by the Josef Fritzl's of this world, rather than being left in a shallow grave and not knowing what type of tortuous death that they had endured. Personally, I'm not sure which is worse a fate. One where it's over and done with, or where you have to keep hoping that someone will eventually come and find you.

Her parents actually took it rather well. I think they were grateful that we hadn't forgotten Rosie, and that we were still trying to find out what had happened to their baby girl. Anyway, for now, it's a case of waiting, and this is something that I am not very good at! The team is using some sort of radar device to image the subsurface of the soil. From what I understand, if the body is wrapped, it is more likely to be discovered as it provides a reflective surface. It's a funny feeling, that on one hand, I would love to be right, but on the other, it would mean that poor little Rosie will undoubtedly have met a gruesome end.

Josephine

"Oh my god, Mum! What has happened to you?"
I limp into the kitchen; I can feel blood streaming from my nose.
"I'm not really sure, darling, I was walking in the woods and I saw that Pierre chap. You know, the one who has taken a shine to the girls. You know… I mentioned him to you, he always says 'bonjour' when he sees them. Anyway, I walked past him, and he was saying something that I didn't understand, and then, I don't remember anything else. I must have tripped and hit my head because the rest of it is a bit of a blur. I then woke up on the floor, and now here I am… Oh my, look at the state of my new trousers. I've ripped them…."
"Never mind your trousers, Mum. Look at your face! Did he do this to you?"
"No, darling, don't be silly."
"Well, I think we should report it to the local police. Maybe he attacked you!"

"Police! No Shelley! Leave it!" Just then John walks in. "What's happened?"

"Mum has been attacked!"

"What? Attacked by who? What's happened? Did you see who did it? Did they take anything?" …. He has clearly switched into police mode, and he is now asking me numerous questions. I half expect him to get out his pencil and pocket notebook, and begin to take my statement!

"Look! No one has attacked me. I was just out for a walk, I tripped and I fell!" I say this exasperated…

"…That Pierre was there at the time of this trip and fall apparently …" Shelley tells this to John.

"He always gives me shivers that one."

"What one?"

"You know, the old man who is always outside the 8 à Huit. I think that he must be a drunk."

"Oh him! No, he's not a drunk. Shelley, he's got dementia. Marie told me when I went to pick Maggie up that time." John pipes up with this info... but Shelley is still not convinced...

"Well, I still think he's a danger....and I think that we should go to the police...."
"And say what, Shell? Look, Josephine, were you attacked, or did you fall?"
"To be honest, I can't quite remember, but I think it is more likely that I fell."
"Ok... Well, let's get you cleaned up, and if any memories come back, and you think that he did have a hand in this.... then we can report it. OK?"
"Look, I don't think that any memories will, and I would rather leave the police out of it. Anyway, I'm fine, it's nothing...."
I say this as I make my way into the bathroom, and I begin to study myself in the mirror. I have a sudden flashback to Pike's murder, and how I looked after that night. It was a moment of déjà vu!

DS Rachel Cooper

That first day was very long, and completely fruitless. Nothing even remotely had been discovered to suggest that little Rosie Flood had even been there, let alone been buried! They have now started to take soil samples to see if they can pinpoint a better location, and narrow down the search area. Apparently, as bodies decay, they affect the pH of the soil. Although in theory this sounds good, in practice, I'm not so sure. Her disappearance was over three decades ago, and surely if she is buried there, she would almost certainly be skeletal by now, so what decomposition fluids would still remain? I wished that I understood it all more, but I was never really any good at science. I only managed a Double D at GCSE, and even that was by a complete fluke!

John

I go into the village to pick up a loaf, having already used up the last of the bread for the girl's breakfasts. I had kissed both of them goodbye at the school gate, and they had happily skipped in. I cannot believe just how well they have settled in. Heidi was really picking up the language. I wish my brain was a sponge like theirs, I am still struggling with just the basics. Luckily for me, the locals are desperate to practice their English with me, otherwise, this sabbatical would have been even harder. I am really missing my job, and I have yet to find any sort of work. I know it's not exactly critical yet, but I have always been the breadwinner and this stay-at-home Dad lark, is a whole new experience for me, and I'm not entirely sure that I like it!

Shelley and her mum were up and out early again this morning. They really do seem to enjoy picking the fruit, and it does actually sound quite fun. Had it just been me and Shelley out here, I would have definitely joined in. However, it is not and I don't want to intrude on their mother and daughter time.

Anyway, this morning there is a lot of rushing about in the village. I pop into the Boulangerie to pick up a loaf, and there is a very animated conversation taking place in the queue ahead… "Cet homme est dangereaux!" Even with my school-boy French, I had understood that they had said: "the man was dangerous!" When it was my turn, I paid my money, having pointed to what I wanted and I asked Dominique, the Baker's wife for an explanation…. "Do you know who they were talking about? They were saying something about a man being dangerous?"
"Yes …" She replied in English, in her very elegant French accent.
"They were saying that Pierre is a danger to the public…" Pierre? I was pretty sure that was who Josephine had seen yesterday before her fall…

"Isn't it Pierre, who is always outside the shop?"

"Oui, the same… He is not really a danger; he is just ill. He just needs our help… And now he is missing! That is why it is so busy in the village. They are sorting out a search party."

I start to feel immediately sick. Shit! Has Josephine done something to him? *She carries on…*

"Apparently the Farm Workers are out looking for him…"

"Ok, well can I help? I'm, Um… I used to be a police officer."

"I'm sure you can. Speak to Pascal. He is heading up the search."

She points through the window at a very tall man dressed in a Police Nationale uniform. I leave the shop immediately to go and speak to him. All the while my head is pounding. I have an internal dialogue going around and around…. *I knew you couldn't do this. She's a fucking serial killer John! Why the fuck didn't you just arrest her when you had the chance? And now... you dickhead... She has gone and done it again!*

"John, John..." My thoughts are interrupted as Dominique calls out from the bakery door behind me.... "You forgot your bread!"

I turn back and I thank and apologise to her, as I take the baguette. I then continue again towards Pascal. I have to tell him what I know. It may seem a little bit premature, but I am convinced that she has done this. I can feel it. He's speaking on the radio. He's got a very deep French accent, and I can't make out one single word. He finishes what he is saying and then he turns to me...

"Puis-je vous aider?"

"Um, parlez vous anglais?" I say hoping I've remembered it right. I'm feeling really rather stressed, and what little French that I did know, has now instantly evaporated.

"Yes, how can I help you?"

"Ah great, my name is John and I'm a British Policeman. Your man, Pierre who is missing. I think that my mother-in-law is involved."

"Do you live up at the White House?"

"Yes, yes, that's right we are renting it."

"Yes, two little girls, your wife, and her mother?"

"Yes, yes… Well, she, I think is involved. You see, she saw him yesterday… in the woods."

"Yes, yes… I know already. It was on the radio."

"Oh my god, so I am right! I knew it. I'm so, so sorry, I thought I had this under control…." He cuts me off mid apology…

"Sorry? Don't be sorry, she is the one who found him. He is already in the ambulance…." My stomach lurches… Ambulance!! *He continues...*

"He had got lost overnight. He has got, how do you say? Déshydratation?"

"Dehydration?"

"Yes, that's it, but…." I cut him off.

"So, he is alive?"

"Yes, he is alive!"

"Oh good, I am so pleased…. Sorry I don't actually think you need me after all…"

"No, I don't suppose we do…. But I thank you, British Policeman, John!" He says this with a smile. I'm not sure if he is taking the piss, but I really don't care! I walk away from him and back up to the house. I'm in total shock, I was so sure! I go to the kitchen and I take out a beer from the fridge. I know it's not even 10:00 am, but I really need a drink.

DS Rachel Cooper

There has been no news from the marshes. The experts are still doing what experts do, and I know that I could sit up there and watch, but to be honest I'm meant to be on a rest day, and I really do think that I could be more productive elsewhere....
I decide to pop to the gym, after all, it is all about work-life balance, isn't it?

Anyway, I'm halfway through a spinning class, and I have really started to feel the burn. I try to distract myself by looking out through the glass walls of the studio, and I see Stu. He has only just arrived. I can tell by his swagger as he comes through the foyer. He has absolutely no hint of any exertion yet...not like me... the sweat is flying off! He is busy chatting to a couple of the staff. He really does seem happier these days. Maybe this separation from Kate is actually a good thing.

I'm then forced back into the zone by the instructor hollering at me. "NUMBER ONE... COME ON... PUSH IT, PUSH IT!!" and I'm immediately propelled into peddling faster...

"THAT'S RIGHT, WELL DONE, FEEL THAT BURN!" Feel the flipping burn... I'll be on fire if I push any harder!! After another 15 minutes of complete torture, the class is thankfully over, and I actually feel numb down there. I also realise that I have adopted a John Wayne gait!

I go to the changing rooms to have a shower, and as I'm about to leave, I see Stu again through the gym window. He smiles and waves at me, making his fingers to the shape of a T. I nod my head and make my way to the Café. After about ten minutes or so, he walks in... "Ah good, you got what I meant... I couldn't work out how to make my hands into a C for a coffee!" I laugh, and he takes a seat at my table.

Shelley

Mum and I get back home after another long day. It has been unusually hot for the time of year, reaching a sizzling 28 degrees. I walk into the kitchen; it is a mess, and I can see at least six empty beer bottles on the side. I walk through and into the lounge. The girls are happily doing some colouring-in at the coffee table, and John is fast asleep on the sofa. I see another empty bottle, which he has discarded on the floor. Given how much he has clearly drunk today, I'm amazed that he had even remembered to pick the girls up from school, but I'm grateful that he has. He stirs and I can smell the stale beer on him.

"Had a good day?" I say with a slight barb to my voice….
"Yes actually." He slurs back.
"It looks like you have had a party…. And I see that you didn't get a chance to tidy up the breakfast things."

"No sorry, I've been a bit busy." He says this whilst wiping the sleep away from his eyes. I don't comment, but my annoyance at him is starting to grow.

"Where is your mum?"

"She has gone for a bath. She says that she has got a backache, so she could do with a soak… and phew… it has been hot out there today …" I say this whilst waving my hand about quite dramatically as if it is a fan, just to illustrate the point…. However, not that John would have known… that really was the beauty of the stone-built Gite, it never really warms up inside. Great in the Summer, but heaven knows what it will be like in the winter months! I continued …. "And we had quite a delay this morning. That Pierre, that attacked Mum, he was missing, so we were all out searching for him."

"Yes, I heard… Isn't your mum the hero of the hour? I heard that she was the one who had found him?"

"Yes, she did, he was deep in the woods …. So, what is going on with you? How come you are in this state?" I say looking down at him as he is still horizontal on the sofa.

"What state?"

"Um, drunk! Really drunk! I've seen all of the bottles and well... you stink!"

"That's not fair. I've only had a few... I just needed a break."

"From what, John? You don't do anything!" I'm hot and tired and annoyed at the state of the place...

"That's a bit uncalled for.... I got the girls up and to school. I bought some bread, I've picked them up, and now they are even doing an activity, and not just glued to the telly..."

I realise that I am probably being a little bit harsh, so I leave it there. I don't want to have an argument, but there is definitely something wrong. He is hiding something. I just know it.

DS Rachel Cooper

The midday coffee has turned into an all-day event. I had no idea just how much I enjoyed Stu's company. I knew that we had gotten on well when we had been back on Team together, however, I had just put that down to him simply having the patience to show me the ropes. He was different and didn't just bark orders at me. He wasn't that much older than me either, even though he had decidedly more service. I think after doing the maths, that he must have joined straight from school. He was also much more relaxed lately than I had ever seen him. I really do think this split is doing him the world of good. I know that it is doing me some good too. I actually think that he is flirting with me! Anyway, we had finished our third coffee and neither of us had wanted to say goodbye.
"Are you hungry?" He said.
"Yes, actually, but I don't fancy anything from here…"

"No, me neither… Um… do you fancy coming back to mine… I could rustle us up something?" I didn't need to think about it… I straight away replied, "Yes great, that would be wonderful…" There was no point playing this cool.

We walked out to the carpark… "Are you going to follow me?"

"Follow you?"

"Yes, so that you know where you are going…"

"No need, I know your address…"

"Oh ok… have you been stalking me?" He says this jokingly…

"Nope… I'm a Detective. It's John and Shelley's, isn't it?... I know it well."

"Ah OK, are you friends then…?"

"Um, something like that…. Look, I'll meet you there. I have just got to get something first."

"OK, no problem. See you in a bit."

DS Rachel Cooper

I decided to go to Stu's via home. I had got showered and changed at the gym, but I'd forgotten my deodorant, perfume, and makeup, and I wanted to look my best. I had had such a great morning. I am just leaving my flat, and I see that there is a bottle of red in the wine-rack…. "That will do nicely." I go back inside to pick it up.

With the bottle now under my arm… I am finally ready to leave. Rosie Flood then pops into my head. I had realised that I'd not thought about the case all morning. I must have been really enjoying myself. I drop Kev a text message.

Any news?

He responds almost immediately…

No, none and my budget is burning up, we might have to abandon this one! ☹

He puts a sad emoji face at the back of his message... funny... I never thought that he was an emoji kind of a man!!

I drive the 15 minutes over to Stu's. I can't believe it, but I've never actually been inside. Ma'am, had made Shelley's arrest on the original case and I wasn't involved in the search. It's a lovely looking house from the kerb, well-kept, and homely. I park up in the driveway, just behind Stu's car. He is another one who has new wheels. I am pretty sure that the firearms lot actually print their own money!! Stu sees me and comes out of the porch to meet me....
"Ah... so you found it then?" I go to join him and he leans in to kiss my cheek.
"You look nice..."

I was a bit taken aback by the kiss. I know we are definitely colleagues, and definitely friends, but are we moving towards something else? I wasn't sure but I really hoped so…. He spies the bottle of red, and takes it from under my arm.

"Ooh lovely, I'm glad you stopped off. I was just thinking that I'd got nothing in for us to drink…"

I follow him into the house and a warm comforting smell greets me… "Mmm, what's cooking? It smells amazing!"

He smiles and laughs… Actually, it's my speciality… jacket spud!"

"Ah, lovely… I like a good oven-baked potato. You just can't beat it!"

"…that and some left-over chilli. It's the only thing that I had in the fridge."

He opens the fridge door to demonstrate and yes, other than a half pack of grated cheese, there is literally nothing. You can tell that he is living alone.

"Um… Stu, do you mind if I use the loo?"

"Not at all, you know where it is…"

"No actually, can you point me in the right direction?"

"I thought you'd been here before, when you said that you knew it was John's place…"

"No… I've not been here. I was just involved with Shelley's case…"

"Ah I get-cha, yes that was a royal fuckup. I think they are going to be getting some compo over that."

"Yes, I believe so… Sorry Stu, the loo?"

"Ha sorry, straight up the stairs. You can't miss it!"

After about five minutes, I'm back down, and I go into the kitchen.

"The spuds need another 10 minutes. Do you fancy the guided tour?"

"Actually yes… great idea, it's a lovely house, it's got a good vibe."

We do the downstairs, it's pretty standard. Kitchen-diner, playroom, and lounge. There is absolutely nothing personal that has been left out. It's furnished, but no pictures, knick-knacks, nothing. I instinctively open up one of the drawers in the dresser, but it's empty.

"You're not on a job Rach, you don't need to search the place!"

"Sorry Stu, instinct… I can't believe how clear everything is. You would never know that this was their home… Or that you lived here for that matter! Where is all of your stuff?"

"Still at home… I've got some bits in the bedroom, but this all came out of the blue. I had been doing that much overtime; I just didn't realise how unhappy Kate was. Although, to be honest, this separation is probably no different for her. I was never really there anyway. It has impacted on me the most, as I have now got to do my own washing and cooking. It's a bloody nightmare!" He says this jokingly. "Anyway, enough of all that… Let me show you the upstairs and then we can crack open that red."

"Perfect!" I say as I follow him up the stairs. "Well, that's the bathroom, that's the kids' room and this is mine!" He points into the master bedroom. It is at the front of the house and overlooks the tree-lined street. It's lovely. On the bedside table, he has got a picture out, which is of him, Kate, and the kids. In fact, this room is the only one that actually appears lived in. It also reminds me more of a teenager's room. The bed is unmade and there are dirty clothes in the corner which are next to the wash basket and not in it!

"Oops, I should have given this a tidy before I did the tour!" I laugh at this comment, and I reply … "It's fine, mine is the same…" I lie…

"Ah, so you play netball with your dirty boxers into the wash basket too?" This makes me smile… He is so funny!

We then turn to leave his room, and I notice another flight of stairs. "What's up there?"

"Ah, that's a strict no go area. It's their loft. I think they were at some point going to make it a conversion, but it's in no way finished. Anyway, it's got all of their stuff up there. I had a quick peek when I first moved in, but John specifically asked me not to go up there...Health and safety, I think..."

"Ah, ok..."

"Right then, are you hungry! Does Madam fancy my speciality of Cordon Bleu Chilli?"

"Well, when you say it like that, how could I resist.... I'll pour the wine!"

We had an absolutely fantastic afternoon. After lunch, which was delicious by the way... we had then sat together in the lounge. The weather had turned, and the rain was cascading down the front of the sash windows. I was totally relaxed as was Stu. He was sat next to me on the sofa, and I had my legs tucked up underneath me. He grabbed my hand. "Do you know what, Rach? I've had a brilliant afternoon. Thank you."

"Ah, you soppy sod. You don't need to thank me…." He then leaned in and quite unexpectedly he kissed me on the lips. My whole body fizzed, and it felt amazing!

Josephine

My back is no better. These days it seems to permanently ache. It actually reminds me of period pains, but as I have already been through the menopause, it really can't be that. I can only put it down to that fall in the woods. I also feel exhausted at the moment too. I think that maybe I'm a little late in my life to have started manual labour, especially in this heat. Shelley and I are the only ones who are covered in suntan lotion, wear hats, and with all of our arms and legs covered. You can totally tell that we are related. We only need to look at the sun and we are burnt. I take a couple of ibuprofen for my aches and get I back to loading the truck.

Shelley

John, actually seems a lot more relaxed after his all-day session. I'm not sure what was up with him, but he is definitely much happier. He also now has a job. He has started doing deliveries for the local shop. His French isn't really up to much, so he was quite limited over here in terms of his choice of job, but navigating google maps and driving, he is an absolute pro at. He must have been worrying about the money, that is all I can put it down to. Not that we really need much out here. Stu's rent covers the cost of the Gite and the mortgage at home, and Mum and I, we cover the other costs, food, etc.

This really is the life. I am loving the fact that we are no longer over scheduled. Before all of this, every night the girls were at this club or that. I (before my time in prison) worked all the hours in the day (and often the night), as did John. I had absolutely no idea just how little quality family time that we really had. Now we eat every meal together and we go for long walks. I have also realised that I no longer have the need to run to calm my anxiety. It has all but disappeared, and I know that is wholly due to having my mum around. I am so happy; I wish I could bottle this time and keep it forever safe.

DS Rachel Cooper

Oh my god! They have found a body…. Not just their remains but an actual body…. I'm not holding out too much hope that it is little Rosie, as surely if it is from thirty-four years ago… she would be bones? They are busy processing the scene right now, and then they are taking it back to the lab… I may not have been right about Rosie, but at least someone is going to get closure soon and discover the final resting place of their missed loved one.

John

I have decided to let it go. I will still try to keep an eye on Josephine, but I can't be monitoring her 24/7. In fact, it is an actual impossibility. I will have to take comfort that she is rarely out of Shelley's sight. After all, they work together, we all live together, and what real motive or time has she got to kill anyone else? I was a little worried about Pierre, but she was the one to have actually found him. There was nothing sinister, he is just the local madman; every village has one and on that particular day, he had got himself a little lost in the woods....

I have also taken on a little delivery job. It's nothing special, and certainly not taxing, but it was really killing me not earning. I am so used to having my own money, and although we really aren't spending a great deal over here, it is still important that we are not using up all of our savings. It's always best to be sensible and keep a little back for emergencies, you never know what is just around the corner. I really wish Shelley's compensation would come in soon. What do you think being wrongly convicted and imprisoned is worth these days? £500K? God, I hope so!

DS Rachel Cooper

I am so impatient, I know I am and I don't mean just with work, I mean with every aspect of my life. The lab is slowly and I mean very slowly processing the body. They have said nothing official yet, but from what I gather it could be little Rosie. They had confirmed that what had been recovered was definitely a female, and she looked on initial observations, to be approximately the right size and age of our missing girl. What we have found is really quite interesting, as is the biology behind it. And it explains why they have found a body and not just her skeletal remains as I had expected...
Apparently, with marshes and in particular with bogs, because they consist of mainly decayed vegetal matter, this can inhibit the decomposition of any organic material. This, I have learnt is because of the following factors...its constant wetness, acidity, and anaerobic conditions. I had been impatiently grilling Graham ahead of the report. He had replaced Shelley, as our

Head of Forensics and he had been trying his best to explain it to me in layman's terms, but he wasn't really doing a great job. So, I resorted to Google. From what I can make out, the moss (that likes these conditions) acts as an antibacterial and therefore it will help to stop any decay. This coupled with the cold water, and the lack of oxygen, will then in turn limit the role of any insects, (who would normally be integral) in breaking down the tissues and proteins in the body. So, if I have understood it all correctly…in a nutshell, it's probably the worst place in the world to have disposed of a body at…. And so far, what we have managed to retrieve is some clothing and a body with actual skin!!! The skin had been stained brown due to the soil, so initially, I had thought that the poor soul that had been discovered, was not our little Rosie who was IC1. But now that I understand it all a little more, it is extremely exciting… And all of this is down to me and my hunch!!

Things have also been hotting-up with Stu. I have probably accelerated that too. I just really enjoy being around him and the sex!! OH MY GOD, the sex! He knows exactly what he is doing. I think if I were Kate, I would have put up with the work hours, just for the multiple orgasms… I feel a slight tingle down there, even thinking of him…. Never mind, her loss is definitely my gain!

DS Rachel Cooper

I have stayed over at Stu's a lot recently and that photo of him, Kate, and the kids is no longer out on display. He seems to have got a lot better at netball too, as there are hardly ever any pants left on the bedroom floor. There is also now food in the fridge, and wine in the rack.

I feel like everything is going my way for once. I have a boyfriend, (yes, I said it...) I know technically that he is a married man, but you can't have everything... He has even got kids already, so he won't be expecting me to produce any for him, and what's better, he doesn't want me to meet them yet. He is trying not to unsettle them... So, as I am not the maternal type, this really is the perfect scenario! I know that I sound like I am getting ahead of myself, but it all feels so right. He could actually be the one!

Kev is also walking around the station like he is the cat that got the cream. We are still no further on in terms of getting an official ID, but he feels justified at having spent most of our budget on the search team. I think he was getting a little hot around the collar at the beginning of all of this, him having focused the search on my hunch alone. We work so well together, and I really feel like he is in my corner. I can actually envisage my next promotion. I have already taken the exam, and this is the perfect evidence that I will need for an Interview Board. Detective Inspector... Ooh, I like the sound of that!

DS Rachel Cooper

So, I'm over at Stu's and we've just eaten a lovely dinner of steak and thick-cut chips. I have also guzzled my way through most of the Merlot. Stu goes to pour himself some, and a single droplet falls into his glass. "Enjoy that did you?" He says.
"Um… yes actually, it was really nice. There's another in the rack…."
He goes over to the far end of the kitchen to look, and shouts back to me… "Erm, no there isn't, I think you drank that last night!"
"Sorry Stu, look, I'll go and get another…"
"I think not young lady, I'll be arresting you for drink-drive if you do…"
"Ooh, I hope so! Will you use your handcuffs and your gun?" … I'm starting to feel that we should forget about the wine, and carry on our role-play upstairs, when he says "Look, I really do fancy a drop. I won't be long; the shop is only a five-minute drive. I'll be back before you

know it, and you never know…. I might even find my cuffs!" He says this with a wink.

He gives me a lingering kiss on his way past, and he's off out the door. Bloody typical! He gets me all in the mood and then he disappears. Left on my own, and ever the practical one, I decide to wash-up and await his return. However, rather annoyingly, when I move over to the sink, I manage to get the edge of my top into the bloody pan. We both like our steak medium-rare, so there are quite a lot of meat juices still remaining. I curse as it's new. I whip it off, taking it upstairs to the bathroom sink for a soak, (the kitchen one is still full of the washing-up that I was just about to tackle…. Grr!)

Anyway, whilst en route to the bedroom to get myself another top, I see that the loft door is ajar. I know that this is a no-go area, and that curiosity always kills the cat, but that didn't stop me… I went up the stairs and in through the door. I could completely understand why John didn't want anyone up there. It was literally packed to the rafters. There was box after box, but rather helpfully each one was named. I couldn't quite see down the far-end as the light was very dim, but that didn't matter as the boxes closest to me clearly had "Josephine" written on them. I picked up the first box and took it down the stairs to the bedroom. I quickly pulled on a top, and then went downstairs to my handbag and I got out a pair of search gloves. I was that type of copper, who was always prepared. I saw on my phone that I had a text from Stu.

Shop closed, going to supermarket…. will be a bit longer xxx.

Perfect! I thought to myself, I've got a bit more time….

So, there I am back in Stu's bedroom with the first box in front of me… I was so excited. I felt like a kid about to open her presents on Christmas morning. I take everything out, carefully inspecting what each item is.

There is a teddy bear, a child's watch, a beer mat, bible, pencil-case, old school books, a crucifix, etc. It looks like lots of personal memories, and mainly from her childhood. My first assessment is that there is nothing of note, and to be honest, I still didn't know what I was looking for. It's just that I have this feeling that she's involved in those murders. Possibly even the Rosie Flood case. After all, she was in the photo in that newspaper article. I feel it, she is connected. My hunch over the marshes was right, we had found a body. So maybe I might just hit the jackpot again here too!

I am totally engrossed in my task and I have forgotten briefly all about Stu, and I don't hear him come home. He's obviously not found me in the kitchen, so he's rightly assumed that I would be in the bedroom (although not for the reason he thinks!) He walks in holding two glasses, and the newly purchased bottle of red. His smiling face immediately shifts to anger as he takes in the scene.... My gloved hands, the box with

Josephine written on it, and the contents strewn all over the floor….

"What the fuck is all this? In fact, don't tell me…. I can work this out for myself... Been snooping, have we?"

I look up at him… "It's not what it looks like…"

"Like fuck it's not! So, has this been your elaborate plan? Orchestrate a relationship with me, make me give up on my marriage, and all so that you can get a look at their belongings…. I thought you'd helped get her off. I asked around after you said you were involved in the case. You were integral in getting Gordon done…. So, what are you up to now?"

"Look, I'm sorry, this is not what it looks like, it's just I know that she, Josephine that is, is involved in my cold case. I feel it in my gut. Kev thinks I'm obsessed and so I would never get a warrant…"

"So, you thought you would screw me to gain entry instead? God, you are a cold-hearted bitch... I was actually thinking about telling Kate, and introducing you to the kids this weekend…"

"No, it's nothing like that, I do like you. In fact, I think I love you…."

"Oh, fuck off Rachel, the only thing you actually love is the fucking job! Look, you need to go…"

"Give me a few minutes, I need to pack my stuff up, and then I'll leave… Look, my top is in the sink in the bathroom. Please, can you grab it for me?"

I get up from my task to show him that I am packing up my stuff and he goes off to get my top. I take this opportunity to quickly put the remaining bits from Josephine's box, that I haven't had chance to go through into my bag. (Thinking that I'd have a proper look at these later…) Anyway, after only a minute or so, he is back in the doorway and still clearly fuming, as he throws the sodden top at me. "Here you go…" He has a good aim, as I feel the water droplets bounce up and hit my face, as it socks me on my chest! He then starts shovelling all the bits that remained on the floor from Josephine's box, back inside it, and then he closes the lid. "Right, I'll take that!" He makes a show of picking it up and putting it back into the loft. After a minute or two, he's back in the bedroom doorway. I'm sat on the bed.

"Haven't you gone yet?"

"Look, I'm sorry, can we start again, I was having such a great night. I really like you..."

"I thought you loved me?!" He says with a huff.

"No Rachel, you can go. Whatever this was, it's over!" He picks up my bag... and I briefly panic as I think he's going to search it…. He doesn't. He just takes it down the stairs and straight out through the front door and porch and chucks it out onto the driveway. "Go on then, off you pop!"

He won't even look at me, and there is nothing I can say. I really do like him, but I think I have blown it. What the hell have I done? Why did I not just take a leaf out of Anna and Elsa's book and just let it go?

John

I wake up, it's morning. I see that I have had a text message from Stu, asking if it was a good time to call? It was sent at 23:55 hours. God that was late, I wonder what it could be? I hope the bloody squirrels aren't back in the roof, I don't need anyone rooting around up there... I decide to have breakfast first and get the girls ready for school. I will call him later.

Shelley

Mum comes into the kitchen from the annex and today we are having a well-deserved day off. I have decided that we are going to have a pamper day. Spend some time in the pool, sauna, and hot tub. I have also bought some face masks and a cucumber. We are going to have the full works. All that is missing, is some scantily-clad male masseuse!! Although, knowing Mum, she wouldn't let one near her anyway! She has never had a massage apparently or even been to a Spa. She really does have so many wounds that have still yet to heal. What my father did to her all those years ago was inexcusable. He has negatively impacted upon her whole life. I haven't pried too much, but at the trial, I learnt that she had never even had a relationship. I feel for her as she has never known what it is like to be loved; I know she had a crush on Barnaby when she was a girl, and yes, I know that she had the love of her father, and now the love of me and my girls, but that butterfly feeling in your tummy and that pounding in your chest. That feeling of actually being in love, it is second to none.

Anyway, she is stood before me in her dressing gown with her swimming costume underneath. "Right, shall we have a cup of tea first, and then get this over with?"
"Oh Mum, you make this sound as if it's a chore. It's meant to be relaxing…"
"Sorry darling, I am sure it will be. It's just I have never had a pamper day and I don't know what to expect…."
"Well, I thought we could have a swim in the pool, dry off on a sun-lounger, read a book, drink some fizz… I have even got some cucumber for our eyes; it might get rid of some of the bags under yours!"
"Shelley, you are cheeky… it's a good job I know you don't mean it!"
"Ha, I do actually Mum…You do look tired. Are you sleeping ok?"

"Yes, I'm fine, I'm just a little weary. I think it's all this lugging of plums. I'll be glad when we have finally picked them all!"

We drink our tea, and then make our way down to the pool. This place is idyllic. Jeanette is so lucky actually owning the place. I wonder if she would take an offer on it, once of course, my pay-out comes through? I have spent that money over and over, and I still don't know what I'll get. I truly hope that it would be enough to pay off our mortgage and there would still be enough for a little place out here. Even if it's not this one.

Mum takes off her robe, and I see for the first time just how much weight she has lost. This "manual labour" that she keeps going on about has really helped her shed the pounds. Although, by no means was she big before, she was maybe a ten to twelve dress size, but now she is definitely an eight. I say nothing as I am a little jealous. I have the opposite problem. I have piled it on, even with working on the farm. I think it is finally being content, and indulging in the endless supply of cheese, wine, and croissants that has done it!

DS Rachel Cooper

It's the next morning. I had driven home from Stu's last night. I know that I shouldn't have done. If I had been stopped, I really could have got myself arrested! I think that the shock of being thrown out by him, had sobered me up. Therefore, I had completely forgotten about the three-quarters of the bottle of wine that I had consumed. I only really remembered about it this morning, as initially, I could not work out why I had such a thick head… Obviously, now I realise it was the hangover!

I have a shower and try to eat a piece of toast; I feel shocking, but I am not sure if that is the alcohol or the fact that I feel guilty over what happened last night. I dial Stu's number to try and apologise but it goes straight to answerphone. I then send him a text…

I am sorry. Please call me x

For a brief second, I feel better that I have at least made contact, but then I start to worry again and I begin to feel sick. I know that I need to put this right.

I'm sat at my kitchen table and then I see that my overnight bag is still in the hallway. I go and get it, and put it onto the table in front of me. I find another pair of search gloves and start to pull out Josephine's remaining stuff. I decide to finish what I had started last night.

John

I call Stu, his mobile is switched off and so I try the house phone. Luckily, the landline and the internet were still connected. He immediately picks up...
"Hello..."
"Stu, is that you?"
"Um, yes, it is. Who's that? I didn't know anyone had my number here..." *He questions me suspiciously...*
"It's John, you wanted me to call?"
He takes a big intake of breath.... "Look... I'm sorry John, but something happened last night. I wasn't sure if I should tell you, as there is no damage or anything, but I couldn't sleep. So, I thought that it was the right thing..."
"Well, that's a bit cryptic.... What has happened? I am sure whatever it is... it can be fixed? Although you said no damage.... Sorry, Stu, what has actually happened?"
"Well, I was seeing someone and ..." I interrupt him...

"Look Mate, I don't care who you see, it is your place, you pay rent, you treat it as your home…"

"That's the problem. I was treating it as my home and well, I had Rachel over… and when I came home, she was looking through all of your stuff…"

"What? Rachel who? What stuff?"

"Rachel Cooper…" My mouth goes dry….

"Stu… What stuff? There is nothing in the house. It is all up in the loft…"

"Yeah, sorry Mate, she went up there, and she pulled out a box and was going through it…"

"What box, Stu?"

"It had Josephine's name on it…. Don't worry, I have packed it all back up and it's now in the loft again."

"OK, um, did she say what she was looking for?"

"Some evidence for a cold case… Look… I threw her out… but I am so sorry." I take a breath…

"No, it's fine, there is nothing for her to find anyway. It's just stuff from her childhood, I think. But the bloody cheek of it all. If she wanted a look, she should have got herself a warrant… I didn't even know that you were an item…. When did that happen?"

"It has not been long to be honest, a couple of weeks. I met her at the gym, we got chatting and one thing led to another, and well she's fucked me right over. I can't believe that I have cheated on Kate." I can hear a hint of sadness in his voice…. I have worries of my own, but I feel that I have no choice but to listen….

"Since we were married, I have never even looked at anyone else. She then says that she needs a break and so I give it to her, and then I find out that I am quite fun, and I like having this time on my own… I got chatting to Rachel, and she seemed to genuinely like me and well… she's a good shag and …. you know the rest…"

"Look, don't beat yourself up, no real harm done. Kate and you are on a break that was her idea, and so she can't really hold it against you…. Although don't volunteer it. Only tell her if she asks. As for Rachel Cooper, she is a product of Gordon. It was only a matter of time before she would follow in her footsteps…. Thanks for letting me know anyway, and really don't worry. No harm done."

"Ah thanks, Mate. I feel so much better telling you."

"Yes ok, alright Stu, I have got to go…. I think I can hear Shelley calling me…"

"Ok, see you, Mate."

With that, I end the call…. Have I really nothing to worry about? I just don't know…

John

I'm sat looking out of the kitchen window and I can see Shelley and her mum by the pool. They are laughing uncontrollably over something, but I am not sure what. I really don't know what to do over the Rachel Cooper thing. I am pissed off that she had the audacity to come into my home, and effectively burgle the place. I also don't know whether I should ask Josephine about what was in those other boxes. I know about the photo of Beachy Head, but what did that really prove. It didn't necessarily mean that she killed those men and staged their suicides? And yes OK, she was interested in that paedophile case at the Barrister's Chambers, Bragg or Briggs, or whatever his name was… but again, there is no actual evidence that she was involved. What I need to know, is what cold case Rachel is working on at the moment, or whether she is still unofficially looking into the cases that Josephine has already been eliminated from.

I drop a text message to DS Paul Bacon. He is not in Cold Cases, but he'll know what's happening. He keeps his nose to the ground that one. I immediately get a response back.

Long-time mate, I thought you were on a sabbatical?! Anyway, it's the Rosie Flood case, Misper. They think that they have found her body!

Rosie Flood? The name rings a bell, but I can't quite place it. I pull up Google on my phone and type it in the search field. Immediately lots of old newspaper articles pop up, but nothing about a body being found, so it can't be public knowledge yet. I then look at the search result images to see if there is anything else that would make Rachel interested in Josephine again... Then I spot something...It is a photo of the missing girl in a local newspaper covering the library's Readathon, and I see her. It's a much younger Josephine in the background of the shot… Ah, so maybe that is why she is digging around!

DS Rachel Cooper

I go into the office. Kev has texted me and said that he needs to see me. I immediately forget about Stu and Josephine. If he's called me in for a meeting, this has got to be something good. I walk into the main office area and I can see Kev at the far end. He beckons me over. I go over to him and acting all jovial, I say…. "Alright Kev, how are you?" "It's DI Smart today, Rachel…" His tone is definitely off… "Come on then, I need a discussion with you in my office." Now, I immediately know that I am in trouble. It is not the request for formality, nor his tone but the fact that he wants the conversation in his office. Kev hates it, as he dislikes the divide that it represents. He always says that he sees us as one team and therefore he does not see the need for it…. Today, however, he has clearly changed his approach, and by the negative body language that he is displaying towards me, I really can't see that this chat is going to be about my promotion. Nope, this is definitely something bad.

Shelley

I absolutely love spending time with Mum. She had finally got into our Spa-Day, and when the girls had got home from school, she even painted their toenails for them! It was a little messy and you can see that anything like that is completely alien for Mum. Self-care, it seems has never been high on her list of priorities. Anyway, we are having tea together and her mobile phone rings. It's a number withheld.
"Are you going to answer it, Mum?" I ask her as she is stood holding the phone and looking at the display.
"I don't know who it is. I don't think anyone has my number other than you and John, and well, Probation … and Mary; she usually rings from a mobile number…."
"Well, you won't know who it is, unless you pick it up…"
I do understand her apprehension. After the trial, she was hounded by the press, and she had to change both her house and mobile numbers… She does eventually pick it up, and as she does, she takes a deep breath…

"Hello, yes that's right, Josephine Gilling, yes that's it, yep, 1965… Oh OK…" I can see her face physically whiten.

"Ok then so, next week and you have sent me a letter to my home address? …. OK, yes, I will… See you next week…. Err, thank you." The call ends and she looks completely in shock.

"Mum? Who was it?" She doesn't seem to hear me, so I repeat myself….

"Sorry darling, um, that was…. Err…Probation. They need me to go back for an appointment…"

"An appointment? What appointment? Why?"

"They didn't say. They said that they have sent a letter and that they need to see me."

"Ok, well… It's probably nothing to worry about…"

"Yes, hopefully… Um, I am feeling rather tired. I think I'm going to nip back to the annexe for a nap. Do you mind if I don't help you with the washing up?"

"Not at all Mum, you go and have a rest…. And Mum, don't worry, it will all be fine."

Mum looks back at me and smiles but I can tell that she is worried, and in all truth, so am I.

DS Rachel Cooper

I wasn't in there long, but as soon as he started talking, I knew exactly what the issue was. Someone had made a complaint that I had acted unlawfully, and I had conducted an illegal search of their premises; and what had made it worse, was that they were actually alleging burglary! They stated that I had trespassed and potentially removed some items, equalling theft! Now…. I knew that my intention was never to steal, as such, but if you looked at it purely from the facts, I was bang to rights, as the 'stolen' items were currently sat on my kitchen table. I obviously denied the allegation and said that I had gone up there, as I thought that I had heard a noise. I followed this up with the fact that I had had absolutely no intention, to permanently deprive them of any of their property. All of which, however, fell on deaf ears, because as soon as DI Smart heard who's address, I had entered, and who's property I was interested in, he had made up his mind... I was bang out of line!

"For goodness' sake! I gave you a lawful order to leave that alone. She may have committed the other murders, but you finding the evidence outside of the law renders it completely inadmissible... It helps absolutely no one. I honestly thought that you were nothing like Gordon, but you really are cut from the same cloth. Yes, we all want results, but we get those results lawfully!" I hang my head; I had just become too focused and my tunnel vision had let me down... It was the Shelley Jones scenario all over again!

"... and this isn't the only incident... I know that you went to her flat too... all caught on CCTV. Did you know there had been a spate of burglaries at her block? The DS had come to me and asked what you were doing on the CCTV. He was worried that they might have been stepping on our toes.... I obviously found out what you were doing there... I called the agent. Looking to move, are you?!" I can hear the anger in his voice... I know that I have disappointed him...

"Look Rachel, I don't want to do this, especially as you have made such good progress in the Rosie Flood case, but I need to suspend you. The complainant is considering whether he wants formal action taken, and because of this, I can't have you anywhere near a live investigation."

I understood, of course, I understood, but in the last 24 hours I had managed to lose my boyfriend and now my job, and the only person I could attribute all of this to was Josephine bloody Gilling. She really was my nemesis. She was at the heart of Gordon's destruction and now she's at the heart of mine!

John

I have packed a bag and I am going back to the UK with Josephine. I have told her that I have some loose ends to tie up at work, and that her appointment is perfect timing. Although, in reality, I am only going back to make sure that she is ok. If needs be, I will call Larry or that Isaac chap. I can't work out why probation want this meeting. What do they know? Is this Cooper's doing? If it is, I am sure that they will be interested in her antics. This could even be a case of harassment as well as the burglary. I still haven't told DI Smart what I want to do about her illegal search of our home; but for now, the fact that she is suspended is enough for me.

DS Rachel Cooper

I have been through so many emotions this past week. Anger, frustration, bitterness, infuriated, mad…. Since my suspension, I have been to the gym every day and practically beaten the punch bag off of its chain. That fucking bitch, she gets off with a poxy suspended sentence for killing an innocent man, and she also manages to carry out at least another three murders. I even heard that the other "CJ", the brother who was her actual rapist, turned up dead with no explanation. She then swans off to fucking France, without a single care in the world. Kev did at least assure me that if there were any links to her, he would follow them up but that was it, I was out of the loop, and I still didn't know if it was Rosie's body. I am annoyed at myself too, as I feel like I have really let the parents down. I felt a connection to them both and if it turns out that it is her that we have found, I wanted to be the one to have told them.

I have heard nothing from Stu. He didn't return any of my texts or calls. I have even driven past his address a couple of times and have not seen the car in the drive. It's all so fucked up. I've lost everything!

John

So, we took the Eurostar to St Pancras. Neither of us had felt much like driving, and so the nearly six-hour train journey from Bayeux, actually didn't seem too bad. Isn't that what they say? "Let the train, take the strain." It was the perfect time for me to read the book, that I had been meaning to finish for months, and to catch up on what had been happening in the world, as I relaxed listening to a few of my favourite podcasts. Josephine however, she did none of these things and she was even quieter than usual. This journey was nothing like the convoy of us travelling to France that second time... On the ferry there was such a buzz... Shelley, her mum, and the girls were just like charged atoms, all stuck together as they explored the boat and discussed what they were going to do over there, once we were all unpacked and settled. This journey in stark contrast was very subdued…. This appointment that she had with the Probation Service; it had really unsettled her. I don't know what they had said to her, but for long periods of the journey, she had just kept looking out of the window and staring vacantly into the far distance. I had just got back from the buffet car with a croque-monsieur for both of us and coffee, when she turned to me and said "John, do you believe in karma?" It was a strange question to come out of the blue like that ... but I responded... "Well, I believe in justice, if that's the same thing?" She acknowledged my answer but then said nothing further ... "Why do you ask anyway?" "Oh no reason, I just wondered, because I think I do..." "Oh, OK? Anyway, eat it up whilst it's hot..." She didn't bother with the food, and nor did she say another word to me until we were back in London. It was very strange, almost as if we didn't know each other. We were just like two commuters sharing the same table seat. You would never have known that we were related.

"So, did you manage to get hold of your friend, Stuart? Is he OK with you staying at the house? Otherwise, the offer of my sofa is still there…"

"No honestly, it's fine. Actually, he texted me and said the house is empty at the moment. He is giving it another go with his wife…"

"Oh well, that's good then…"

"Well not really, if she takes him back, we've lost a tenant!"

"Oh John!"

"I'm only joking, of course, I am. I've known them both for years. Much better together than apart. Anyway, so I'll be staying at the house. Do you want me to see if I can borrow Jeanette's car and run you to your appointment tomorrow?"

"Oh no! It's fine. I'd rather go alone!" I was shocked at how panicked that she had sounded when I had even mentioned going with her…

"Oh, OK, no problem. I didn't want you to think that you were on your own." A little calmer now, she replies. "No, it's very kind of you. I don't want to be a burden..." I thought it was a strange thing to say. I wondered what she thought they knew.

Anyway, after taking the tube and the mainline train, we were finally at our destination. As we were about to part, her getting the bus up to her flat and me walking to the house, she came towards me for a hug. I instinctively responded. Even knowing what I thought I knew, I still felt drawn to her because she and Shelley were so alike. And as I affectionately squeezed her, I understood what Shelley was talking about. She had said that her Mum had lost weight, and I could feel it, she was practically skin and bones.
"Ok, well let me know how you get on..."
"Yes, will do, I'll see you later."
"Oh, and Josephine, don't forget your phone, and if you need me... just call."
"Yep, promise... thanks, John!"

… and with that, she had got on the number 66 bus and she was away home. I in turn walked my way back to the house. It had actually taken no time at all, and as soon as I had put my key in the door, and had switched on the kettle, there was a knock at the door. It was Jeanette… A great neighbour when it comes to emergency babysitting, or letting you use her Gite for gratis, but giving you any privacy, nope…. she was absolutely rubbish at it!

DS Rachel Cooper

I feel like a bloody leper, no one is returning my calls. I just want to know what is happening. I won't get involved; I won't undermine the case, but I need to know… Was the body Rosie Flood's? How long does it bloody take? We had taken her parent's DNA, so surely it would be easy enough to confirm it one way or the other? Anyway, I'm sat here in my flat, and I'm going out of my mind… this was all down to me and I'm being shut out! I also drove past Stu's marital home the other day. Over the past week, I have seen nothing of him at the gym, nor his car at Shelley and John's. Anyway, I noticed that his car was parked up on the drive, so he's clearly gone back to her! It's just not fair, none of this is my fault. It has all gone so wrong.

I reach over and pour myself another glass of red. I know it is only midday but what does that matter. I'm suspended, so I may as well spend my time doing something that I enjoy!

Josephine

It had been a long journey and I was exhausted. After the bus ride, I had trudged along the pavement towards my block. I was greeted by a black cat that walked across my path… I couldn't remember if that was lucky or not, but either way, I felt that my fate was already sealed. I put my key in the main door and walked up the steps to my flat. Having turned the key in the lock and opened the door, I embraced the familiar smell inside. I went straight into the lounge room and after collapsing on the sofa, I just sobbed!

DS Rachel Cooper

I wake up, my mouth feels dry, and I can see that I have a number of missed calls and messages. All telling me to watch the news. I had felt my wrist vibrate a few times as my watch notified me, but I was so disoriented after having finished off the bottle, that I had thought it was my alarm clock. I knew that I didn't need to get up for work, so I had ignored it... Anyway, true to his word, Kev had messaged to say that the ID had come back as Rosie; but he had also told me to watch the news. He was so by the book. He would never be the one to give you the inside story... So, I pull up my BBC news app and I cannot believe what I am reading. They had not only found little Rosie's body, but also another missing girl from around the same time, a Stacey Saunders. She too was six, but according to the papers, they had thought that she had been abducted at the time by her father, and was now living abroad. There was absolutely no hint that she had been murdered. It was no wonder that the lab had been slow with confirming the victim's ID, I expect that they had uncovered Saunders first. I read on further and apparently "Official Sources", Kev, they mean, "...believe that the girls were both murdered around the same time. They already have a suspect, so for now, they are not looking for anyone else." OH MY GOD... I was right!! It was Frost. He bloody well did it!! I immediately put a call into Kev. It rings once and then goes straight to answerphone... Damn it, I really want to speak to him and find out a bit more. My impatience gets the better of me, so I decide to call Debbie. She is the office gossip, and what she doesn't know, isn't worth knowing... I know I shouldn't really be calling her but needs must!! She answers immediately.

"Oh, Hi Sarge... are you feeling any better? The Gov said you'd got a bad case of flu or something... I bet you are gutted not to be in, it's all going off here!"

"Oh, yes, the flu. Terrible one; worst I've ever had..." I try to hide my initial confusion as to why she thought I hadn't been in. I think that my response must be worthy of a BAFTA nomination, as I had quickly put in a cough. She then asks me…

"What can I do for you anyway?"

"Well, I was trying to get hold of the Gov, is he there?"

"No sorry, he's permanently tucked up. This meeting and that. Since the story broke, everyone wants a piece of him… Terrible, isn't it? Those poor girls. Have you seen their pictures; they could actually have been twins?!"

"No, no I haven't, I've been a little out of it…"

"Yes, flu can do that. You need hot lemon and lots of rest… Ooh and chicken soup. My grandma Betty, she swore by it…"

"Yes, yes… thanks, Debs…" I want to steer the conversation back on to the investigation, but unfortunately, we have now got stuck on the topic of my wellbeing, as she continues to reel off numerous home remedies for flu……

"Do we definitely know it was Frost?"

"My goodness yes! … I would have thought that the Boss would have told you that… but you know… He raped them too… the clever forensic lot, they have uncovered semen in the clothes that they were wearing at the time… Poor little things. Only six-years-old the pair of them…" It made me feel sick, just hearing her say it. Those poor babies, even I felt for them and I didn't have a single maternal bone in my body! I had no idea how their parents would take it. I just wished that I wasn't bloody suspended and I could actually help. I thanked Debbie for the info, and she wished me better soon. After the call, I then text Kev.

Boss, look I know what I did was wrong, and I'm sorry, but please let me come back. You need me.

I then pressed send and all I could do was wait for his call, and his open arms. My hunch had really put Cold Cases back on the map, and the big bosses would definitely now be leaving our budget alone!

Josephine

Last night I hadn't slept a wink… I wasn't sure if it was because of the sleeping bag that I had borrowed from Shelley (my bedding was in France), the fact that I was hungry (I hadn't been able to stomach a thing) … Or that today, (and most likely the reason) was the day of my appointment. I was up early and after having made myself a black coffee, I had tried to eat the stale croissant that Shelley had packed up for the journey. I looked out into the garden. I was desperately searching for my robin, but I couldn't see him. There was no reassurance visit from him today….

Anyway, after having showered and dried myself off with the microfibre towel, another thing that Shelley had given to me. (It was the size of a postage stamp, but it actually seemed to work!) I got myself dressed, and I found the letter that I was told about on the phone. I left the flat to catch the bus into town. The journey was anything but relaxing. My appointment was at 09:00 am, so I was sharing the bus with a number of school children, and the harassed commuters trying to get to the station in time for their train. It was therefore very noisy, and there was lots of pushing and shoving. The only good thing about it, was that I was so occupied with what was happening around me, that I didn't get a chance to think about, what was waiting for me ahead. Once I had arrived, I went straight to the main reception area, to get directions to where I needed to be. The young receptionist had a pleasant manner, and once she had seen my letter, I saw a flash of sympathy across her face, then she said… "Take the lift and go up to the second floor, and then follow the blue line. It's then the second door on the left… Make sure you book in at the reception. You don't want to be recorded as a no show!" I thanked her and then I made my way towards the lifts. I had a dreadful feeling about this. I just knew that my time with Shelley was going to be cut short. I had a sixth sense that I wouldn't be returning to France.

John

It was actually lovely to be back home. Don't get me wrong, I really love being in France and being with the girls, but it was also nice to be back in Blighty. An Englishman's home is his castle after all...

After Jeanette had spotted me last night, she had immediately come over to check on Shelley and the girls. She even popped in some leftovers for my dinner. I had a thoroughly enjoyable meal of Shepherd's Pie. I hadn't eaten anything like that for months... She had asked how we were getting on at the Gite, and what our plans were long-term. I didn't really have an answer for her, but I said I would have a chat with Shelley when I got back to France. If I didn't know better, it sounded like she wanted to sell the place. Anyway, for now, I've got to sort out Josephine and the issue that she has clearly got with Probation. I really hope for Shelley's sake that it is just a misunderstanding.

Josephine

So, once I have booked in at the Second-Floor Reception, I am told by this rather officious woman to go and sit outside of Room 2b.   Instantly I think of Shakespeare.   I feel so ill-fated.

John

I've not heard a word from Josephine. I would have thought that she would have called me by now, but nothing. Shelley had already rung through, and I had spoken to the girls before she took them to school. It was rather handy that the plum picking season was almost at an end, as Shelley and her Mum were no longer needed. My bosses at the shop, thankfully were happy for Shelley to cover my delivery job, for the few days that I was away. They were so accommodating.

Anyway, so after the third time of Shelley calling me, and asking for an update that I still couldn't give; I decided that rather than wait for Josephine to get in touch with me, I would take the bull by the horns and ring her myself. I didn't want Shelley to call again and for me to still not have any news. I was already in trouble with her, for not having gone with her mother to the appointment.

I selected her number from the recent call list and pressed the green button. Her phone simply rang and rang, she didn't answer. Maybe Shelley had had the same thing happen, which was why she was bugging me... Anyway, I tried again but she didn't pick up. So, I decided to check on her location. I had installed this software onto her phone before giving it to her. I know technically that it was against RIPA and her Human Rights, but this wasn't for a job, this was for Shelley, and my own peace of mind. I wanted to ensure that she didn't lose her mother again. I pulled up the software and I couldn't believe what I saw. The map had a pin in it, and she was nowhere near the Probation Service Offices. What on earth was she up to now? I immediately put on my trainers, and left the house, going straight to her location.

Josephine

I felt like I had been assaulted and I could not believe what I had just been told. It still needed confirming officially, but from what I gathered, it wasn't good news. The information that I had initially been told was incorrect, and therefore it seemed unlikely that I would be returning to France. I felt broken, how could I tell Shelley? She was going to lose me all over again. This was all so unfair!

John

So, I make my way into town, and I then catch the bus by the station, and I travel to where the map had pinpointed Josephine's position. It thankfully wasn't near any woodland. I at least had comfort in that, but I still wanted to know what she was doing there.

Josephine

I take the lift back down from the second floor and I make my way out into the reception area. I see the young girl over by the desk. She looks up as I walk past and she smiles at me. I'm not sure if she remembers me from earlier, but I smile back anyway. I'm a little distracted, so I don't see this tall male coming towards the desk and we end up colliding.

"Oh sorry, I was so fixed on finding the reception, I didn't see you there..." He says to me...
"It's OK, no harm done...." I reply... And then we both look up at the same time having recognised each other's voices...
"Josephine?"
"John?"
"What are you doing here?" We both say this at the exact same time...
"Well, I, um… I came to see someone."

"Oh OK, well I'm here to see someone too, you know I told you, I had some loose ends to tie up… Remember? I said?"

"Um… yes I think so…" Just then, the young receptionist comes over to me, and she says…

"Did you find the Ultrasound Department ok?"

I begin to colour up… "Um… Yes. Thank you… Thank you for your help…" She then turns to John… "Can I help you, Sir?" John looks uncomfortable at this question.

"Um, yes, I'm a police officer and I'm looking for one of my victims…"

"Oh, OK. Well, I'm sorry, and it's not that I disbelieve you, but could I see your badge? We get all sorts of nutters in here…" John appears really uneasy at her request.

"Well, I don't actually have one at the moment. You see, I am on a career break, but I had a few loose ends to tidy up…."

"Well, I am sorry then, I just can't help you. Maybe get one of your colleagues, who is not on a career break to come and I might be able to help…" It's John's turn now to go red, and he stutters (something I have never seen him do) and he then apologises to the receptionist, and then he goes to leave. He seems to have forgotten that I was there.

"John! Are you ok?"

"Yes, sorry Josephine, are you? The Ultrasound Department, doesn't sound like somewhere where you would visit someone?" I can feel my face flushing again…

"Well, no, no it isn't."

"Look, do you want to grab a coffee? My work here is done."

"Yes, ok, that would be lovely."

I was so pleased to have actually bumped into John, him being there had really forced my hand. I needed to tell someone, I had to confess.

John

I couldn't bloody believe it, I walked slam-bang into her. I really thought that my cover had been blown when the receptionist had wanted to see my warrant card… I could tell by her face, that she thought I was a nutter. I suppose what police officer, goes to see a victim wearing a hoodie, shorts, and trainers? Never mind, at least Josephine didn't seem to question it, so I suppose that was the main thing.

Anyway, we went for a coffee straight afterwards, as I could tell that there was something up. She had the same tell as Shelley. The right corner of her eye, it twitches if she isn't being truthful. It was actually a good job that I hadn't stopped at the coffee shop on the way to the hospital, as I had only taken my Oyster card and paper money out with me. The bank card, that I thought I had in my phone case, I had obviously left on the side and the paper money was euros, and certainly not what today's Brexit Britain would even remotely entertain as currency! Anyway, so she treated me to a coffee and a slice of Victoria sponge cake. Another thing that I hadn't realised that I had missed until now! We sat down in a window seat; it was her choice. It's not normally where I would choose to sit, and certainly never in the middle of town. The terror threat is real you know… But as she had already slumped down, I felt that I shouldn't insist on us moving.

"Are you ok? What is really going on with you?" She looks up at me. Her eyes are glistening with tears and she begins to speak…
"What I'm about to tell you, you cannot tell Shelley, at least not yet. But they think, they think…" She begins to sob and she cannot finish her sentence… She looks so much like Shelley, that my heart begins to race. All I want to do is protect her.

"Please Josephine. Continue." I reach out and hold her hand, and at this point, she takes a deep breath and begins to speak...

"Well, it's just…. before we went to France, I had been having some issues. You know woman's things. So, I went to the GP to get checked over, blood tests, etc. Anyway, they told me that it was nothing to worry about, and that everything had come back clear. They had put a lot of my symptoms down to anxiety because of the trial and it was just my body's way of coping with it…" I nod my head as I listen to her…

"So, anyway that call the other day. Well, it wasn't probation, but actually my doctor. They had tried to contact me several times on my mobile and landline, but as you know, I had to change my numbers and I had forgotten to update them. So, they had been to my address as they had sent letters and I hadn't responded. I didn't bother with a postal redirection, as I thought there wouldn't be any point. I do most of my stuff online…" I am listening, but she is taking a very long-winded route by way of getting to the punchline… I try to stay focused.

"So um, the Doctor went to my address and as luck would have it, the Estate Agent was around showing a potential tenant, and him obviously not knowing anything about data protection, he has given over my new number… and the rest I suppose they say is history…"

"What is history? You haven't told me why you were there? You're not pregnant, are you?"

This immediately breaks her clear sadness, and she laughs! I realised just how silly my question had been, but I still needed to know what is going on.

"But that receptionist, she said ultrasound?"

"Yes, she did… look, the blood test at the Dr's showed that I was high with CA 125. That is an indication of ovarian cancer. I was having the ultrasound to confirm a diagnosis."

"Oh Josephine, I am so, so sorry. So, what did they say?"

"Well, the nurse that performed it, she didn't say anything. She said that I'd need to see the Specialist. But I could tell by her face…"

"Look, you don't know anything for sure yet… And so, this whole thing with Probation?"

"Untrue. I didn't want to worry Shelley unnecessarily and it was the most plausible excuse…. Anyway, so why were you at the Hospital? Are you sick too?"

"No, no, nothing like that. I really was looking for someone…"

"Oh OK…"

"So, what now?"

"Well, I suppose I have to wait, but it looks like I won't be going back to France for the foreseeable…"

"Well, no, but I really do think that you should tell Shelley. Good or bad, she has missed out on so much time with you, I think she would feel cheated if you kept this from her…"

"Isn't that what Mothers are supposed to do? Protect their children?"

"Well, yes. But not in this case. In this case, I think she would want to support you. Look, I'll let you think about it. But I know Shelley."

Josephine nods her head as she finishes her coffee. Her cake is left untouched on the plate.

"Are you going to eat that?"

"No, it's yours, take it…"

DS Rachel Cooper

I have heard absolutely nothing from Kev, and it's been at least two days. I feel a bit happier in myself, as I managed to limit my wine consumption last night. I am trying to be healthy, so I have gone to the gym. As I walked into the foyer, I bump straight into Stu and then Kate. So, my assumptions were right, they are back together. It was a little awkward, as I hadn't initially seen her and my face, having seen Stu, it had lit up. "Stu! How are you?" His face was not so beaming. "Oh Rachel, you remember Kate, don't you?" I turn and I see his wonderfully trim wife, walking just behind him. She clearly clocks my initial look of joy at having seen her husband, and then also my disappointment at seeing her in tow.

"Um… yes… How are you, Kate?"

"Very well, thank you. I am just spending some quality time with my husband…" The frostiness in her tone made me immediately think that she knew about us…

"Look, I'm so sorry about what happened, it was only a fling really and it clearly meant nothing…" Stu looks at me, he opens his mouth but nothing comes out… On hearing my apology, Kate seems to spin her head, it was like something out of a horror movie… and she spits out the following words, her anger clearly apparent…

"Are you bloody kidding me, Stu? You and her?" I immediately realise my mistake, as the look on both of their faces says it all.

"Shit! You didn't know. I thought he had told you and that was why you weren't overly friendly…"

"What with the bitch who has been shagging my husband?!!" Stu tries to quiet her down, and he begins to speak to her in a hushed tone…

"Kate, look, shhh… You are making a scene. It's nothing like you think…"

"Oh, do enlighten me… How was it then?!" She shouts this at the top of her voice, before planting her fist firmly in the middle of his face. He is clearly taken aback as he stands there for a minute shell-shocked.

She then turns and walks off, and out of the foyer... and not even a minute goes by; I am still stood there open-mouthed, next to Stu... when I see and hear his brand-new car driven off at speed, screeching as it does.... Stu still hasn't said a word. He is just clutching a bloody nose.... Then a member of the Reception Staff approaches him, she is holding a tissue out for him to take.

"Sorry to disturb you, but that was all captured on CCTV. Would you like me to call the police?"
"Um...it's fine... There has been enough dirty washing aired today, I don't need to be the talk of the Station too." She looks over at him, clearly not understanding what he has meant...
"So, do you want me to call them?"
"No, no I don't." *(His voice is frosty in its tone.)*
"Ok, no problem, well if you change your mind, it will be on tape for 30 days..." He thanks her, now remembering his manners, and then she is gone.

"If only all of our crimes were that easy to solve, you've already got a named suspect, willing witnesses, and the CCTV… It's an open and shut case!"

"Oh, why don't you just fuck off!" He says whilst pushing past me and out of the door.

First my suspension and now Stu, can things get any worse?

John

Josephine and I have parted ways. I have just been to the supermarket to pick up a pack of beers and the makings of a chilli. I did ask Josephine if she had wanted to join me, but she had declined saying that she just needed some time alone to think. She said that she needed to work out how she was going to tell Shelley. I really hoped that Shelley would text me later, rather than call. I was never any good at lying. She always knew when I was fibbing; apparently, my voice had a tell-tale wobble to it…

Anyway, luckily for me, she hadn't called until later in the evening, and by which point, I was well into my pack of beers and any wobble was disguised by a slur. Stu had called me to ask if he could stay. Kate had found out about him and Rachel, and she had kicked him out yet again. We had discussed how similar his scenario was to the TV show 'Friends', and the characters of Ross and Rachel. I had kept saying "You were on a break!" I thought that I was so funny and because I was pissed, I couldn't stop saying it... I still couldn't believe that Kate knew. I had said not to volunteer it, but apparently, they had seen Rachel at the gym, and she had just blurted it out. I don't get that one. I had actually thought that she was quite together, but now from what I know of her, maybe he had a lucky escape... and she is just another bunny boiler!

Kevin Smart had been in touch, wanting to know what my intentions were in relation to the burglary. Before today, I was thinking about letting it slide, but after what she has done to Stu, I am going to let her sweat it for a little while longer.

Anyway, when Shelley called, the conversation went like this.
"John, you sound weird, is everything ok?"
"Yes, why?"

"Um… who is that in the background? Is that Mum?"

"No, no it's Stu…"

"I thought he'd moved out?"

"Well, he had, but he's back now…"

"John, are you pissed?"

"I may have had a few…"

"This isn't a bloody jolly! You are meant to be looking after my mum!"

"I am…"

"Well, how are you doing that? Is she there? I have tried her on her mobile and it's switched off!"

"Look… Shell, calm down. As far as I am aware everything is fine. She had said that she wanted an early night, so that is probably what she is doing. I am sure she will call you in the morning… OK?"

"Mmm… I suppose so! Just don't go forgetting why you are there. I knew that I should have been the one to have come back with her. I've been that busy today too. Kids school run, all of your deliveries, picked them up again, dinner, then bath and bed! I've not stopped and it sounds like you are on a bloody beano!"

"I promise you, it's not what it seems like… I have already fought off the Spanish Inquisition. Jeanette was on at me as soon as she saw me…" I say trying to change the subject…

"In fact, I think she wants to sell."

"Does she? She never mentioned it to me."

"Why, when did you speak to her?"

"Yesterday, she knew you were coming back and wanted to know your favourite meal… How was the Shepherd's Pie?"

"Amazing actually, ah bless her, she said it was leftovers … Look, I've got to go… Stu is still here and I feel like I am being rude…"

"Ok, well don't forget to tell me what's going on. Love you!"

"Love you…" and the call ends.

"Blimey, Mate! Was she roasting your balls for having a drink?"

"No, not really, it's more because she hasn't heard from her mum."

"Ah OK…. Anyway, what do you think I should do? I know I need to give her some space. Can I stop here for a bit?" I obviously tell him yes, but with the caveat, that it might be only a temporary arrangement. I have a strong suspicion that Shelley's dream of living in France full-time is about to be put on hold.

DS Rachel Cooper

Ok, so now I have really, really fucked up…I didn't even bother going any further into the gym. By the way that the other members were staring at me, I knew that I was the topic of the hushed whispers. I diverted to the corner shop instead. I picked up a couple of dairy milks, and four bottles of my favourite red. (I've gone off the Pinot. You have to wait too long for them to chill!) Anyway, they were on offer, so it would have been silly just to pick up the one. As I go to pay, I see the newspaper. I hadn't checked the news app yet, as I had been a little distracted. Anyhow, it seems that the press had now been given the full story. They had a photo of Eric Frost, alongside the photos of his two little victims. I now knew what Deb had meant, when she said that they looked alike. You could hardly tell them apart. Anyway, the press seemed to have all the facts. It looked like he had raped and killed these poor children, and then disposed of their bodies near his lockup, located on the edge of the wetlands. I was shocked at just how much detail there was. I know we wouldn't be prosecuting, (obviously, because he was dead,) but what if they were to run a posthumous trial. Talk about full disclosure! So, I bought the paper, as well as the wine and chocolate, and I made my way home. As soon as I was in the door, my phone rang. It was DI Smart.

"Rachel. DI Smart here."
"Yes, Sir, I know, I saw your name come up."
"Look, Rachel, I really don't know what you are playing at, but how clear do I have to be that you are suspended?" I try to speak but before I say anything, he continues...
"I got your text but no, I don't need your help and after your latest trick, I am livid! Did you think that I wouldn't find out? You called up Debbie to get the insider info?"
"Well yes, but only because..."
"Because of what? You are not involved, there should be no inside information. You are on a suspension. A

suspension that I stupidly kept hidden, as I thought this would all blow over with John Jones, and I really didn't want it to affect your promotion…. Well, you can kiss all of that goodbye…"

"Sir?"

"Don't Sir me! You clearly don't respect me, otherwise you would have done what I asked of you…. And before you ask… Yes, I have seen the papers! Did you think it was clever leaking that information? The parents hadn't been told about the rapes. It was a closed circle that knew. I have already spoken to everyone on the team, and the only person that I cannot satisfy myself with, is you! Are you trying to teach me a lesson?"

He has been ranting at me for the last five minutes or so, and I have been unable to counter his accusations. Each time that I try, he starts up again….

"Rachel, consider yourself still suspended, and until you hear otherwise, make sure that you stay away from this, or any other investigation. Got it?" I know he won't listen to me, so I just respond.

"Got it." The line goes dead, and there I am, alone again in my flat.

It did get worse.

Josephine

I had had another restless night, but I knew what I needed to do. I just wanted confirmation, one way or another, and if it was the worst-case scenario, I would just do everything in my power to stick around for Shelley and the girls. I felt like I had already survived the worst. What cancer could throw at me, was nothing in comparison to what I had beaten so far. I had never been a victim, and I wasn't going to start now.

Josephine

The call from the hospital had come sooner than I had thought. I was to attend a Specialist Gynaecologist Oncology Appointment the next afternoon. Due to the speed of their response in organising my appointment, it seemed that I definitely had this terrible disease. I just needed to know how I was going to beat it.

John

Josephine called me, and she told me that she had a hospital appointment the following afternoon. She was seeing a Dr George Hail, a Clinical Oncologist. It now all seemed a forgone conclusion. She had cancer. Oncologists, weren't they to do with treatment? Surely, she should have had an appointment first, to be told that she had it, and at what stage? This all seemed very rushed, and from what I knew about the disease, when a hospital is quick to get you an appointment, that is because they feel that they are against the clock. I obviously didn't share this, but I did ask if she wanted me to go in with her. She immediately declined. Instead, she told me that I needed to go back to France, and to be with Shelley. She said this was so that someone was with her, when she told her the news. Josephine had already decided that she wasn't going to go back to the Gite.

"John, it's obvious I have this. I need to be here and, in the UK, so that I have the best chance of beating it."

I couldn't actually believe how upbeat she was. I think the not knowing, was what had silenced her on the train journey over here. Now that she knew what she was up against, and that she could see her enemy, there was no way that she would be a victim. She really did have such a strength of character. It was like Robbie had said that time at the Barrister's Chambers, when she had effectively won her case. You would never have known what battles she had fought…

So, I agreed to do what she asked, and I took the next train back to France. I was instructed that I shouldn't tell Shelley that Josephine wasn't coming too. She would find that out soon enough, when she came to pick me up from the Train Station.

Josephine

My appointment was with a Dr George Hail. MB BCh, BAO (NUI), LRCP & SI, MRCP, FFR RCSI, FRCR, a Clinical Oncologist at the hospital. I had arrived early, and again I went up to the main reception area. The same young receptionist that I had seen the day before, was on duty.

"Good afternoon. Oh hello, you were here yesterday. How can I help you?"
"Wow! You have a good memory... Could you direct me to Oncology, please? I have an appointment with Dr George Hail." Again, I see it, that look of sympathy.
"Yes! No problem... Again, you will need to take the lifts, but this time get out on the fourth floor and follow the red line. You can't miss it. Are you on your own? Was there no one who could have come with you?"

"Um, no, my son-in-law, he offered, but I'm better alone.

"Oh, OK then. Well, you take care, and I hope that your appointment goes well…" I thanked her and made my way via the coffee shop, and then off I went up to the fourth floor. There was another reception, and yet again, as I had done before, I informed them of my arrival.

"Ooh you are very early darling…" said the grey-haired lady behind the desk. "Do you want to go off and come back a little later? He is never early you know. In fact, more often than not, he runs late. He likes to give each patient the time that they need. He is lovely like that, but it does make his timekeeping really rather poor!" I smiled at her, but I assured her that I was fine to wait. "Look, I've got my coffee. I'm fully prepared and I'm sure that there will be some magazines to keep me occupied; there usually are."

"Yes, you are right, and the newspapers. I put them out myself this morning. Ok then, you go and take a seat, and he will call you when he is ready. Oh yes, and if you need the toilet, it's out of the door and over to the right." I thanked her and went to take a seat in the waiting room.

I was actually nearly a full two hours early, but in that time, I had the chance to study all of the comings and goings that went on. I watched every interaction that each patient had with him. He came to collect them, and he even delivered them back to the waiting room. He clearly cared and wanted to support his patients as much as he could. I studied his form, his face, his demeanour, and I decided that I very much liked this man. In between my watching and listening, I also thumbed my way through the 'Hello', 'Cosmopolitan', and even the 'Good Housekeeping' magazines. I didn't bother with the papers, I had a feeling that today was when I was going to get enough bad news of my own, and I really didn't need to read about anybody else's woes.

Josephine

"Josephine Gilling!" I have been called by the good doctor. I raise my head, and I look straight into his hazel eyes. "Hello there, you've been here a while? I thought you were here with one of my other patients. If I had known, I would have tried to see you earlier, to have stopped you from an anxious wait… Come with me then." I do as he says, and I follow the tall, and sandy-haired doctor into his office.

"Take a seat, please. Right then Miss Gilling, do you know why you are here?"

"Well, to be honest, I have guessed, but nothing official."

"Oh dear, I'm so sorry about that…" He starts looking at my notes…

"Right, I can see why you have been given a fast-track appointment. Ok, so far… you've had blood-work done, and an ultrasound. Right, so from initial observations, I am sorry to inform you that all indications are that you have advanced ovarian cancer, so…" he continues talking at me, and I could see that his mouth was moving, but I didn't hear a single thing after the words…. 'Ovarian cancer'…

"As I say, it looks like this is quite advanced, so I would like to book you in for a CT scan and a biopsy. We have a slot available for tomorrow morning. So how does that sound?" I just look at him.

"I know that this is a lot to take in. To make you feel a little more at ease, the biopsy is a relatively minor procedure. We do it keyhole these days. You'll not need an overnight stay, and once it is done, along with the CT scan, we will know what we are looking at. From there we can put together a treatment plan." I feel like my heart is pounding through the walls of my skull and I still can't speak.

"Miss Gilling, are you OK? It is best that we move quickly on this." I finally snap out of the trance that his words had catapulted me into.

"Sorry Dr, just so that I understand. I do actually have cancer then?"

"Yes, and I think from looking at the ultrasound, it is my initial assessment that it is likely to be stage 4."

"And that is serious, isn't it?"

"Well yes, all of it is serious, but this is more advanced than we would have hoped. We just want to do a little more investigative work, so that we can make sure that we decide upon the best possible treatment plan."

"Umm, am I going to die?"

"Well, I need to be honest with you, and to put it bluntly, without treatment, we are looking at six months. With treatment, however, that could be up to five years."

"Six months?"

"Yes, but that is without treatment. Look, let's get you booked in for tomorrow's procedure, and then we can take the next steps, as and when we need to...OK?"

"OK?"

I had already imagined the worst. It was all I could think about, but it was strange having had it confirmed. How was I going to tell Shelley? I hadn't really got away with anything… This was my true sentence.

John

The return train journey was torturous. It was so much slower on the way back to France. I don't mean that time stalled, or we had gotten stuck waiting for a signal to change, nothing like that. I just meant my perception. It seemed to take double the time. I just wanted to get home, and get telling Shelley over and done with, like you do when you rip off a plaster! The sooner she knew, the more time she would have to adjust to the news. I felt rotten for her. She had only just found her mother, and now she was potentially going to lose her again. I had tried so very hard to prevent that from happening. Yes, I knew we had yet to get a final diagnosis, but at the rate they had rushed all of this through, I knew it was serious.

I hadn't yet heard from Josephine, I knew that her appointment was at 2 pm UK time, so it would be over soon, even if it wasn't already. I kept looking at my watch, and 4 pm couldn't come soon enough. I was willing her to call. I wanted to know the results before I arrived at Bayeux. I knew Shelley, and the minute that she spotted me on that train, pulling into the Station, and I was without her mother, she would want answers.

Josephine

Dr Hail, he was so patient with me and he had answered all of my questions. I would be returning again tomorrow morning. It is funny, I have never really needed any medical care... In fact, in my lifetime, I have only ever been to hospital three times. Once, when I was born, the second, when I gave birth to Shelley, and the third, when they fixed me up after my thankfully unsuccessful suicide attempt... Other than that, my National Insurance contributions were largely unused. I had a feeling however, that all of that was about to change. I was about to get my money's worth!

As I took the lift back down to the ground floor and to the reception area, I got to thinking about Shelley. My eyes began to well up. The receptionist caught sight of me as I walked past her desk. There it was again, her sympathetic smile.

Once I was outside and stood in the Hospital Carpark, I took a deep breath. The day was warm, so the air irritated my lungs and I had begun to cough. I just couldn't catch my breath, then I think the realisation of what I had just been told began to sink in. I began to panic. I felt dizzy. I was going to faint. As I grabbed a nearby signpost to steady myself, an elderly male walked past me, he was holding a bunch of flowers. He saw that I was wobbly and instinctively he grabbed me and, in the process, he dropped the flowers… "Are you ok there duck?"

"Oh yes, sorry, I just need to sit… I was just about to slide down the pole and onto the pavement, when he said... "Look, you can't sit on the floor. There is a bench just over there. Let's get you sat down and then I can get a nurse to help you." He supports me as I go over to the bench, and I slump down on its hard surface. I just about manage to say to him…

"No nurse… I'm fine." I then find the bottle of water that was in my bag and guzzle some of it down. He leaves me on the bench and seconds later he is back, having retrieved his flowers.

"Are you sure about that nurse?"

"Yes, absolutely. I am actually feeling much better, I hadn't realised how warm it is out here, and I'd just had some bad news, that's all."

"Oh, I'm sorry to hear that. Is there anything you want to share? I'm sure there is a phrase for it? Shared and it's halved? Something like that…" I smiled at him, he had similar ways to that of my dad. He always had time for people, and he loved a chat.

"Sorry, I don't want to delay you. Are you visiting someone?" I say this, gesturing towards the flowers.

"Yes, but I wish I wasn't… "

"Oh?"

"It sounds awful doesn't it but I don't mean it like that. I just wish she wasn't in this place."

"Your wife?"

"No, she has already been taken... My daughter." He looks so forlorn at saying this...

"Oh, I'm so sorry."

"Oh, it's ok. There is nothing for you to be sorry about. It's him up there that I blame. He has already taken her mother, and now he has got her in his sights. Cancer." *I could hear the sadness in his voice.* "You should never bury a child, it's not the natural order..." Uncharacteristically, I felt the need to hug this old man. He had stopped to save me, and now, I had an overarching desire to save him in return.

"Oh, look at me, I'm meant to be listening to your troubles, and not the other way around."

"No, it's fine, you have already made me feel better."

"Oh, have I? I am so pleased." *A smile crept across his wrinkly old face.*

"Look, you don't want to be late. Visiting hours aren't that long, and I feel much better."

"Oh, OK. Well, if you are feeling better, I should get off to her."

"Yes, absolutely fine."

"You take care now." He smiled at me as he walked away and back towards the hospital. His fragrance of 'Old Spice' lingered briefly and then disappeared. I found the scent very comforting, sparking another happy memory of my dad. It seemed to give me strength. I didn't need to share my problem to make it halved. It made sense what he had said. At least it wasn't Shelley that was sick. She wouldn't be leaving her babies prematurely, and if it was my time, it was still the natural order. I had been fortunate. I had the most amazing time away in France, and I had made more precious memories in the last few months than I had throughout the whole of my teen to adult life. If this was it? If this really was my penance? Well, I would just have to accept it.

John

She calls me just as I'm pulling in at the Station. I can see Shelley and the girls on the platform. Both Heidi and Maggie are prancing about, clearly excited for our return. Shelley is desperately trying to keep them in order…

Anyway, I know that I shouldn't be, but I'm annoyed at Josephine…. Why did she leave it so bleeding late to ring me? I try not to let her sense this in my tone as I pick up the call.
"Hi Josephine, I'm just coming into the station. How did it go?"
"Is Shelley there with you?"
"Um yes. How did it go?"
"Well, it is cancer but there is hope. So, can I speak to her? I need to tell her…" I can't believe how upbeat she is. I really thought that she would be distraught…

"Sorry, Josephine, so you saw the Dr? What did he say?"

"Yes, John! I've seen the Dr and he said I had cancer. Now can I speak to Shelley please?!"

"Sorry, so you want to tell her now? Would it not be better if I told her myself?"

"No, I want to do it, and as soon as you step off that train, she is going to ask you where I am." *She was right of course, as I could already see her concerned face through the train window, and her mouthing to me.* "Where's Mum?" I knew I had no choice. The doors open and I step on to the platform. The girls immediately wrap themselves around my legs, clearly pleased to see me, so all I could do was hand the phone over to Shelley and watch her face crumple.

"Mum? Where are you?" Shelley went silent as she listened to what was said on the other end of the phone. She didn't cry as I had expected. In fact, she showed no emotion. Then she said. "Ok then Mum, well you take care and let me know how tomorrow goes. Love you." She then turned to me, gave me back my phone, and said, "Come on then, let's get Daddy home. We've made his favourite for tea!"

I was in shock. Had she even told her? Why was she not crying? I tried to ask about the call, but she hushed me. "Not now, I'll talk to you later." I wasn't sure if I was in trouble with her, but on the car journey back to the Gite, it was like nothing had happened.

DS Rachel Cooper

I could not believe what I was being accused of. How bloody dare him! Where did he even get this from? Why would he think that I would speak to the press? I was discreet, I could keep a secret. Yes, I know that I had told Kate about Stu and I, but that really had been an accident! You could never call me a blabbermouth! I had run that scenario through my head so many times. What other explanation was there for her frostiness? What was I meant to think? Anyway, she had kicked him out, he was technically a free agent and so I really can't see how she could hold it against him. And... as for leaking classified information to a journalist.... about any case, and especially this one...I would never... I'd met the parents; I was the one making sure that there were no surprises... Surely Kev would know me better than that?! Ah, fuck him! I'll take this suspension, or flu as he calls it and have a break from it all. It's all bloody bullshit anyway!!

John

It wasn't until the girls were in bed, that Shelley finally spoke to me about her mum.
"Did she tell you?" I was very careful not to give away too much… What if Josephine hadn't even told her? I wasn't going to be the one to spill the beans, if at the last minute she had bottled it and decided not to say. But then, she just came out with it.
"She's got cancer you know?" I nodded my head.
"She's got a biopsy and scan tomorrow, and then the doctor will have more of an idea of what they are dealing with. He then needs to decide upon a treatment plan." She was just so matter of fact, and nothing like the Shelley that I had known over the years…
"Are you ok?"
"To be honest John, I am. My mum said that she was fine with it, so I have to be. She's not coming back

here though. She is going to put her all into getting better."

"Ok..." I still had my concerns about how much better Josephine was going to get. I was sure that she was playing down her diagnosis.

"Although John, I have made a decision. We are going home."

Josephine

Was I in denial? I thought about this question, as I was packing my bag to go into hospital... I didn't think that I was, maybe I had simply processed it. Listening to that old man, it had really made me think. His life was far more tragic than mine, and yes, he may have been fit and healthy, but he was alone... He had already lost his wife, his soulmate... And he was about to lose his daughter. I knew exactly how that had felt. I had fought and won once before; I could do it again. I could do it for Shelley.

John

Once Shelley had an idea in her head, that was it. She had immediately packed us all up, and we were ready to go…. I think the move back to the UK, it had given her something to take her mind off of her mother's illness. I obviously had to call Stu to tell him what was happening, and he had of course, completely understood. He said that he would find digs elsewhere. He didn't think that Kate would be having him back anytime soon… "I think that ship has sailed, Mate!!" We had also let Jeanette know. She had confirmed what I already thought, she was selling up…. She was getting too old to keep maintaining it, and her husband had lost interest. We also decided to pull the girls out of school early, but only by one week. It was soon to be the summer holidays, so they wouldn't really be missing anything. I really felt for them, they had only just got settled… So here we are back on the Ferry; both cars jam-packed, and the mood unfortunately, was just like the waters of the English Channel that day, completely flat.

Shelley

It's like we have never been away. I had messaged a few of the girl's old school friends, and I had sorted out some playdates. I wanted to try and get some kind of normality back for them as soon as I could. Although Maggie had already had a little falling out with Sara. Apparently, she doesn't listen!! It made me laugh when she was relaying the story to me. It wasn't that she didn't listen. She was talking to her in French! Well at least we had achieved one of our objectives by going to France, she was definitely bilingual!

Mum was coming over today, I had offered over the phone to pick her up, but she had refused. "I'm not an invalid you know! I can drive myself!" I didn't argue with her. It was good that she wasn't giving up. She had had her biopsy and the results according to Mum were OK, but I still thought that we had a fight on our hands. It was still hard to take in, but I took her lead. She didn't want to think the worse, so neither would I. It's funny, but the worst was all I thought about when she'd left France to come home with John ... I was so convinced that probation had made a mistake, and that she was going to be locked up. I knew just how unbearable prison was. I was so worried. Who would have thought that her little white lie to save me any anguish, would have done the complete opposite. Cancer, as absurd as it sounds, really did seem the lesser of two evils! Anyway, Dr Hail advised that they wouldn't operate initially, instead, he has decided upon an intensive chemo course to shrink the tumour.

Josephine

I have had my first day of chemo, and I really didn't know what to expect. Shelley came in with me and kept me company for most of the day. She had planned to be with me for all of it. She had arranged that the girls would be over at a friend's house, but they had had a falling out, and so they wanted to come home early. The mother had called for Shelley to pick them up. She had tried John, but he had had his phone off... "Oh Mum, I'm so sorry, I wanted to hold your hand throughout all of this..." I obviously told her not to worry. This moving back home had really unsettled the girls. I felt so guilty that they had packed up their whole lives just for me...

Anyway, I had to have my bloods taken and tested and then they prepared my dosage. I had sat there in the chair, and once they had connected up the IV, I had begun the wait to feel sick. I had looked on every forum that I could find, and although some said they felt nothing, others had advised of the terrible nausea and sickness. They had described the crippling fatigue and joint pain, but I felt nothing. When John had picked me up, (he had insisted) and when he asked me how I felt, I honestly wasn't lying when I replied that I felt amazing. I felt in control of my own destiny.

John

Today I've been in to see HR and the Boss to discuss me coming back early from my sabbatical. They said that in principle it would be fine, but I would need to be security vetted again... I was shocked as I had only been away a little over six months... The HR woman had followed this up with, that if I had been in France for another four months, I would have been required to obtain some sort of criminal records certificate from their embassy too... It seemed madness and such a waste of time (and money). They knew me... Anyway, from what I understood, it was going to take at least three months before I'd be back in the saddle. I would just have to be patient.

Shelley had called to ask me to go and pick Josephine up after her treatment. She had gone to the hospital with her, and had planned to stay all day, but then Libby's Mum had called to say that the girls had had a falling out, and she thought it best that Maggie and Heidi go home... It was a little inconvenient, but I suppose that it was still good of her, to offer to have them for the day. We had asked Shelley's mum and dad, but Colin had been rather cagey on the phone, saying that they had had a long-standing arrangement; and that they couldn't assist. It's weird actually, I thought that once we were home, it would have been difficult to keep them away. However, they have only been over the once, and even then, Patty said she had got a cold, so they didn't stay very long. Maybe they had just gotten used to life without us!

Anyway, I had gone into the waiting room, and as I hung about for her to come out from her treatment, I had been imagining the worst. But it was nothing like that, she was practically floating on air when I saw her. "I don't feel sick or anything, maybe it will catch up with me tomorrow..." It amazed me how unfazed she was. I asked her where she wanted dropping and she said home, only because she didn't want to tempt fate, and if she was OK, she would come by the house tomorrow.

Shelley

It was already mid-morning and quite unusually we had overslept... Last night, I had called Mum as soon as I knew that she was home from the hospital. She had said that she felt absolutely fine. I obviously didn't believe her, so I grilled John at dinner, and even he had said she didn't seem affected by it. She was going back in a week, so maybe as the drugs build-up, it would get worse for her, although of course, I prayed that it didn't.

Anyhow, we were still in our PJ's, when the doorbell had rung. I was busy trying to stop both of the girls from blowing bubbles into their Coco Pops... They had gotten these straw spoon things from when we were away, and they were both playing up. John went over to the front door... "It better not be one of those charity muggers... chuggers I call 'em." But as he opened the door, we realised that it wasn't. It was

Mum. She was looking all bright-eyed and bushy-tailed.

"Good morning, have you only just got up?" She says, looking around at us, sat at the kitchen table. The girls with their chocolate milk moustaches and bed-heads, and John and I not looking much better. "Well, to be honest, yes... I didn't think we'd even see you today. I thought you would still be sleeping off your treatment."
"Well, yes, so did I, but I feel great. It doesn't seem to have touched me. I thought I'd come by and pick up my boxes from your loft. It's great having all of my other stuff back from France, but I'm feeling a bit sentimental. I fancy a little rummage through my old memories."
"Mum, are you sure that you are ok? Is it catching up with you? All of this?"
"Oh darling, I'm fine. No, I've never felt better, it's just... you know what it's like... I'm just feeling a little

nostalgic... Anyway, I've got you and the girls. I'll be fine" ... John looks over... "Ah-hem..."
"Sorry! Yes John, I know I've got you too. I was so grateful for the lift home last night."
"It's no bother. I'm about for at least the next three months. Make the most of it..."
"Oh, I will..." She says...
"Right then, you sit down and have a cuppa with Shelley, and I'll go and fetch your boxes. Ok?"
"Ok, wonderful. Thanks, John."
After about five minutes, John walks into the kitchen, and he is carrying all three boxes rather precariously. I could have predicted what happened next... He trips on one of Maggie's bunny slippers, that she had left out, and all of my mum's precious possessions fly out across the kitchen floor! I immediately scold him...
"John, why can't you ever be sensible! It was obvious that was going to happen!"
"Oh, it doesn't matter. There is nothing breakable..."
John and I immediately drop to the floor and start

putting the photos back into the shoebox, I manage to rescue one of Mum in her school uniform, that was trying to escape under the fridge... and then Mum starts putting her bits back into the other boxes.

"That's strange…."

"What's strange, Mum?"

"I can't seem to see my mum's old tapestry makeup bag. It's brown with pink and yellow flowers on it…"

"Oh? Are you sure it was in there?"

"Yes definitely, I found it at the library when I was getting ready for France. I had misplaced it years ago, so I brought it home and popped it in with my other things…. I keep some of my dad's old stuff in it…."

"Do you want me to have a look?" I start rummaging in the box, but I can't see anything as she has described…. Mum is beginning to fret… "Look it was definitely there, and it's really important to me…" She appears panicked by its loss, so I go over to comfort her…

"Mum, I'm sure it will turn up. There is no point getting in a tizz…. Look, finish your cup of tea and we'll have a think where else it could be …"

The girls had been excused from the table, and were told to go off and play… a few minutes later Maggie comes into the kitchen, looking very sheepish…. She has got something behind her back.

"What have you got there? What have you broken now?" I ask this almost instinctively…
"I've not broken anything!" She says this very defensively in her cute little voice. "I found it like this, it won't open." She then moved what she had behind her back, to the front of her… "Oh… You found it! Thank you, Maggie! …." Mum says this elated… Whatever that bag contained; it was clearly very important… Mum then continued speaking to Maggie… "And have you looked inside?" Mum seems to say this in an unusually harsh manner, but maybe

she is beginning to feel tired, as the drugs are having an effect? Maggie is clearly scared by her tone, and her little eyes begin to cloud with tears... "No, the zip is broken, I didn't mean to... It was just so pretty, it got stuck." By this point, I had put two and two together, and it was my turn to use a stern tone.

"Um Maggie, where exactly did you get that from? That was in Nana Jo Jo's box, and that was in the loft.... You know full well that you are not allowed up there! ... I am very, very disappointed in you!" Maggie tries to say that it wasn't, but I know this is untrue. "Where else did you get it from? No, I am not interested! You! Up to your room.... You can come back down, when you decide that you are going to tell the truth!" And with that, Maggie turns on her heels, and she scarpers up the stairs, with shoulders heaving, and the sound of heavy sobs as she goes...

John

I didn't know what all the commotion was about. I'd left the girls drinking tea in the kitchen, and Josephine going on about a missing bag. The next thing I hear is Shelley erupting at Maggie, and then Maggie flying up the stairs. Knocking straight into me, as I was making my way back down…. She was having difficulty breathing, she was sobbing that hard… "Mu… Mum. Mummy doesn't be… li..eve … m, me.." I could tell that she was in distress, and normally I would never undermine Shelley's parenting, but she seemed so upset…

"Come on, calm down… come with me…" I took her into our bedroom and I asked her to tell me what was going on… After I had pacified her, she had explained, that earlier in the week, she and Heidi had been playing hide and seek, and she had hidden in our room, under the bed. She then said that was when she found it… I obviously didn't know what IT was, but then she explained it was the missing bag. She had thought it was pretty, so she was keen to look inside. However, when she tried to open it, the zip got stuck. She thought that she had broken it and as she didn't want to get in trouble, she had hidden it in her room, under her own bed… "…See, I didn't go into the loft, I know I'm not to." Bless her she had got so worked up. I truly believed her too. I had never seen her that distressed… I told her that I'd tell Mummy, and then I helped her get out of her PJ's, and into the dress that she had chosen to wear… going via the bathroom, of course, to wash away the tears and the now dried, chocolate milk off of her mush.

Josephine

"I'm so sorry Mum, I would never have expected her to go up there, let alone go through all of your stuff. Is the rest of it there…?"

"Umm, I can't be sure if I'm honest. I'll have a proper look later. I only really noticed that Mum's bag was missing because it is so distinctive. They don't make them like that anymore."

"Give it here, I'll try and sort the zip. I think if you rub candle wax on it, it helps." I pull it away from her reach…

"No, it's fine! I'll sort it later." I pop it away in a box and then stack the other boxes on top. I can tell that she's a little taken aback by my actions, even though she tries to hide it.

"Ok Mum, it would have been no bother… Look, you are not stacking those up again to carry them, are you? Let me get some clothes on, and I'll help you take them to the car…

"Ok." I say, as she disappears up the stairs to get ready…. I sit in the kitchen alone waiting for her to return. I take a deep breath. I was just so relieved that I hadn't lost that bag!

Shelley

Mum had given me a wide berth this week. I wasn't sure if it was because of the broken bag, or because she was now feeling the effects of the treatment, but she didn't want me to go in with her...

"Darling, there really is no point... Look it's a lot of waiting around, and there's nothing you can really do to help... I'll just do some reading. They've got loads of magazines to help me pass the time... Why don't you spend some time with Patty, I expect she is desperate for a catch-up?"

But it seemed that Mum and Dad were a bit busy too. I had invited them over for lunch, and Dad had declined, saying that they already had plans. Apparently, they would pop over to see us at the weekend. John had also told me that Maggie had confided in him, that Mum's makeup bag had actually been found under our bed. At first, we couldn't work it out, but when we thought about it further, it had to have been from when that Rachel Cooper had been over. John called and confirmed it with Stu ... That cheeky woman had gone snooping, and had brought my mum's stuff out of our loft and was going through it on our bedroom floor. The bag had obviously escaped under the bed when she was caught in the act by Stu. He was so very apologetic, again! Mind you, it wasn't his fault.... He had said that she was obsessed with connecting Mum to her new case, and to the others that she had already been eliminated from... Although, she is on no case at the moment... I believe that she is still on a suspension following on from her antics here – Good job too!

Anyway, seeing as neither of my mums want to spend any time with me this week. I've got some mummy and daughter time to spend with my own girls, and some making up to do with my Maggie. I still feel so guilty. She had told me the truth!

DS Rachel Cooper

How much longer is this internal investigation going to take? I know that I should be embracing it, after all, I am still on full pay, but that's not the point. I need Kev to realise that I would never speak to the press. So, patience, never having been one of my strong points, I decide to call him. It rings just once and then it goes to voicemail. For fucks sake! …. He's cut me off! Anger instantly bubbles up within me. Why the fuck is he doing this to me? I kick out in a rage, and my bare foot ends up catching the wall… "FUCK IT!!!"

Josephine

So far, I have had one treatment and I felt absolutely fine. I didn't feel tired and I've not been sick. My hair is still thick, and there is no more than usual coming out as I brush it... I have had absolutely no adverse reactions... Maybe my body is stronger than I thought. I've told Shelley that I don't need her with me today. If I feel ok in myself, I would much rather come here alone as it helps me to keep her a little sheltered. I prefer it that way... I've always been a bit of a loner... Anyway, this place is not exactly where I would choose to spend quality time with my daughter...

Today, I took a taxi. I didn't fancy driving myself, or getting squashed on the bus, and believe it or not, the return taxi fare is still cheaper than a day's parking here... It's outrageous!

DS Rachel Cooper

With my toe throbbing for the majority of last night, and me being unable to sleep, I took the only medication that I knew would help. I drank a rather lovely bottle of Merlot. However, today I am regretting it, as I now have the mother of all hangovers and a throbbing… no not throbbing, an excruciatingly painful big toe! … It has also started to turn purple, so I know that I have done something bad… I try to walk on it, but I can't….and I definitely know that I can't drive, so I pull on some clothes and I call a taxi. I unfortunately, need a trip to A&E.

Josephine

It's funny, other than me using probation as my cover story for the phone call, and my reason to return home, I hadn't once thought about Joseph, or anyone else for weeks. In those first few days, I had considered that I had been given this terrible disease as my punishment; but lately, I've come to realise that it just happens. You are not chosen; it is just a malfunction. I had gotten this insight because I have got to know some of the other inmates... (as they call themselves!) Ha!! The irony of it. If only they realised... All of us are here for the same reason... All of us are being slowly poisoned in the hope that it rids us of the demon, but the angel still remains. I look about and I see young and old, all of us in battle. Some, they wear their fight more pronounced, scarves covering lost hair, dark circles showing their insomnia, caused by nightmares and worry. None of which however, have I so far felt. So, if this were a punishment, surely, I would feel this more than most?

Anyway, when I bumped into the DS who was the Officer in the Case for Joseph's murder, I did not feel the need to bare my soul, and to tell her why I was at the hospital….

"Well, well… and there was I thinking that you were on your jollies …did France not work out then?" I was a bit shocked to see her to be honest, and it took me a while to place her. She was nothing like the well-turned-out officer, that had stood beside me and had charged me at the Custody Desk. Today, she reminded me more of what the other detainees had looked and smelled like. She had a tracksuit on, greasy hair, and flip flops. I could also smell the stale alcohol on her breath…

"So, did you know her then?" She said snarling at me.

"Know who?"

"Rosie Flood? Well, you are in that photo… Is that why you killed him?" She was clearly in pain being stood upright, and she, like me had gotten a taxi to the hospital. That was where our brief encounter had occurred. At the taxi rank, both of us coincidentally being dropped off at the same time… I had absolutely no idea what she was talking about, and maybe it wasn't stale alcohol, maybe she was actually still drunk… Anyway, I knew I couldn't be late for my appointment, so I didn't stay to chat… (as friendly and as lovely as it was to catch up?!) I left her to it, she could barely walk, so I knew she wouldn't be following me….

I made my way into the reception area, and over to the bank of lifts and up to the now-familiar fourth floor… Once again, I had to have my bloods taken, and then came the wait for my medication to be prepared. I was just wondering how to occupy myself, when I saw the stack of newspapers in the corner of the waiting room. I hadn't much bothered with the news of late. It was always bleak, or a biased narrative that the media fancied putting out there. What happened to reporting things as they were? Why crop an image to only show half the story or take a quote out of context?

Anyway, as I was fed up with reading about how to make the best jus to go with your Sunday roast, or about which celeb has just had Botox, so I opted for the trusty Gazette. I picked up a few actually, they were all old copies and appeared to be well-thumbed…. The receptionist spotted me taking them… "Oh lovie, they are last weeks… the latest one is here if you want it? I've not had a chance to bin those ones yet…" She came over to me with today's paper in her hand… "Actually, I'm ok. I've not really kept up with the news lately, it will give me a chance to catch up.

Do you think I'll have time to nip down to the Café before the blood results come back?"

"Yes probably, but steer clear of caffeine, remember, it doesn't mix well with your treatment…" I smiled at her; I knew that she was just the receptionist, but she sounded just like the nurse last week…. Maybe there was a book of helpful hints that they all had, and that was listed as number one!

"Yes, thank you… The nurse and doctor have both told me about caffeine…"

"OK… We'll see you back here in a bit. I'll leave this paper here then, and those others… bin them once you are done if you don't mind." I told her that I would, and I made my way back downstairs and into the Café area. I hoped that I didn't see that Rachel again. She really did have a bee in her bonnet about something!

DS Rachel Cooper

I couldn't believe it! What were the odds that we would both be at the same place, and at the same time! I had absolutely no idea that she was even back from France, so why was she there? She didn't look sick, so maybe she was visiting someone...

Anyway, after a very long wait in A&E and an X-ray, it had been confirmed that I had broken my big toe.... The doctor, he was very kind to me, and he advised that rather than using alcohol as a painkiller, I should use the more traditional methods of paracetamol and ibuprofen. Apparently, I need not have come, but they strapped it up anyway. I was told that I just needed to rest it .... He had asked what job I did, and I told him, obviously omitting my current suspension ... "Well, you won't be arresting any criminals for a while." More's the pity I thought, as there is one somewhere in this very hospital. He continued by saying… "Get yourself a desk job for a bit, and if you are sensible, you will soon be up and about, and back on your feet!" I thanked them for sorting me out, and I hobbled my way back to the taxi rank, with of course my supply of the recommended painkillers… How very boring!

Josephine

I had taken a seat with my decaf coffee, and I was just about to binge on the newspapers, when I saw a familiar face. It was the old man with the flowers. I smiled at him. "Hello there duck, how are you?"
"I'm ok thank you, better today... How is your daughter?"
"She's ok, I don't know if I told you, but she had surgery, and she was meant to be coming out on the day after I met you, but she now has an infection so they are keeping her in for a bit..."
"I'm sorry to hear that... Do you want a coffee?"
"Actually, that's exactly what I came in for..."
"I'll get it for you, it will be nice to have some company. You sit there..." I say gesturing to the seat opposite mine. "What do you want?"
"Vanilla Latte, please. It's my daily treat..."

Anyway, his company meant that I tidied the papers away, popping them back into my bag, I'd just have to catch up on the news later.

John

I was surprised when she had called me to be honest. She had seemed to have stepped back from us quite a bit recently. I wasn't sure why, maybe she felt she had to battle this alone. It made her stronger somehow. Anyway, apparently today's treatment had made her really nauseous, and she was worried about being sick in the back of a taxi... What about being sick in the back of my car! She obviously didn't care about that!! So, I did what any dutiful son-in-law does, and I turned up with my seats covered with a black sack and a bowl just in case...

She was stood waiting just outside the main doors, and she did look green... "Are you ok?" I said to her as she got into the front of the car... She smiled at me as she clocked that the seats were covered, and then she shifted her feet to accommodate the washing up bowl that I had brought along with me, for use as a sick bucket… "Yes, I'm OK… I have felt better obviously, but I think I just need to get home."

"Ok, no problem, I'll take it as slow as I can, and if you need to stop, just let me know…and… obviously, if you are going to be sick, please try and use the bowl!"

"Yes, I know…. You love your car." She says trying to smile.

"So not good today then?"

"No, I had a coffee and I think that did it, I had asked for decaf, but maybe they got the order wrong… I feel so rough."

"Well, we will soon get you home."

"Have you had a good day?" I think she asks this more out of politeness rather than actually caring, as she has immediately opened the window, and was now deep breathing out of it…

"Yes, nothing overly eventful. I caught up with an old colleague earlier… and we actually went for a run together… God, I'm old… I chose exercise over a beer!" She is clearly feeling a little less sick as she has now closed the window…

"Oh, that reminds me, I saw that DS today… The one who charged me…" I instantly stiffen…

"What? Here? What did she want? Was she harassing you?"

She laughs… "No, not at all, she seemed drunk. I didn't really recognise her to be honest. She was rambling on about something, but I wasn't sure what. She was in a right state…"

"Oh, OK and she wasn't bothering you?"

"No, I saw her for less than a minute…"

"Ok…" We turn up her road and into the carpark of her flats…

"Do you want me to help you in?"

"No, I'm fine… but can you let Shelley know that I probably won't be over tomorrow. The way I feel at the moment, I don't think I'll be up to it… I'll call her."

"Yes, no problem…" and at that, she has closed the car door. She then fishes around in her bag for her key and she then disappears into the block.

John

I get home, and I can tell that Shelley had already started tea, the smell of garlic and tomatoes immediately hit me on walking in through the door... She is stood by the hob, busy stirring a pan. I go over to kiss her...

"Thanks for doing that love, was she OK?"

"She looked a bit green, but other than that... my seats are still clean and smelling sweet! Which obviously is the main thing!!" She gives me a playful punch...

"Oi! Behave yourself! ... Actually, have you brought back my washing up bowl?"

"Oops, it's in the car, I'll be back in a mo..." As I walk away, she shouts... "Oh yes, how was your run?" After I have retrieved the bowl, I come back in, and we carry on the conversation.

"The run was good actually, it was nice catching up... Oh yes, that reminds me... your mum, she saw Rachel

Cooper today. She was at the hospital apparently…" Shelley bristles.

"Was she bothering Mum? She has got enough to deal with…"

"No, apparently not, she said she was drunk!"

"Drunk? Well, that's strange, isn't it? …. I wonder what time that was?"

"Anyhow, it's got me thinking… Shall I call Kev Smart, and tell him that we don't want to proceed with the case? Yes, her judgment was off, but I think maybe we have let her sweat long enough. She's a bit strange, but she is fundamentally a good copper. It doesn't seem right, that she's not out there catching the criminals…"

"Oh, it's your call John, I don't care either way. I just hope that she leaves Mum alone!"

Josephine

After John had dropped me home, I had just enough energy to change into my pyjamas and to crawl into my bed. I think I must have slept for at least 18 hours solid. I had a number of missed calls and voicemails from Shelley, all concerned that she hadn't heard from me yet... I messaged her back.

I'm fine, just tired, I will call later. Love M x

I then went into the kitchen, and I had a mint tea as I still felt sick, I also tried eating some dry toast... I had sat down at the kitchen table and I noticed that my bag was on the floor, with all of the papers spilling out... one in particular, caught my attention. It was folded over, but I had immediately recognised the eyes that were staring back at me... I went over and picked it up and as I unfolded it, there he was. Old Ferret Face!

DS Rachel Cooper

So, I have had a missed call from DI Smart. I try to call him back, but it goes straight to voicemail. Finally, he rings me and I bleeding well miss it... Typical!

Josephine

I could not believe what I was reading…. How did I even miss this? The headline said FROST YOU CAN THAW IN HELL… As I read on, I discovered that Eric Frost, my second kill, had had an even darker side to him, than I had known. He had actually raped and murdered two little girls. He then disposed of their bodies near his lockup. Immediately the penny dropped! Of course, that was what Rachel Cooper was talking about….

The news article, it named his two victims as Rosie Flood and Stacey Saunders… They had both gone missing in 1986… The papers had described Frost as a cold-hearted man, who had even been charged but not convicted for molesting his own stepdaughter… 'Frost by name, frost by nature'…. The article said that his reign of terror was cut short at the hands of his own wife, who had been convicted of his murder. Yes,

I knew all about that…. Apparently, she was still protesting of her innocence…. Ha!! Maybe of his murder, but not of the abuse, she had to have known….

This news, although sad, it had actually perked me up a bit. I had started to feel a bit unsettled over my past actions. I still wasn't sure if this was karma, and I was now ill as a result… Anyway, after reading this article, I felt surer than ever that I had done the right thing. Those poor innocent little girls. I knew that what I did, although it would never bring them back, at least I had got them and their families justice, and he, over the following three decades, had not had the chance to hurt anyone else… His poor stepdaughter, my goodness; I wonder how she must be feeling. I wondered how close she had come to being body number three?

Anyway, I pick up the rest of the papers, and I scan through them to see if there is any further info, but there isn't … There is just some of the usual rubbish about Brexit and how the Tories were crippling the country. To be honest, it doesn't really matter who is in power, all of them are equally terrible at it! It is only ever about themselves, their pay rises, and pensions! There is no such thing as public service these days… I was a true public servant; I had achieved so much more than any MP ever had, whilst sitting behind their desk at Whitehall!

As I carried on with my research, I switched to the internet… Immediately, a bit more of what the DS had slurred at me at the hospital, had started to make sense. On my first Google search, I had come across a photo of Rosie Flood, and in the background, there was no mistaking it, it was me! I hadn't realised it, but I had actually met her. It was a photo of us both at the library. The poor girl, it can't have been much after that picture was taken, that she would have died…. From reading the various articles, I pieced it all together. He had been working next door to her home address. I felt sad, knowing how he would have groomed her, flattered her. I wondered what he had said to entice her to go with him? Anyway, it was after her disappearance that he, the wife, and his stepdaughter had all relocated over to Essex; running scared, I bet!

I put the name Jodie Frost into Google, and I was surprised with what I saw… One of the papers had managed to get photographs of all three girls. Rosie, Stacey, and Jodie, all aged six and you could not tell them apart. Their chosen headline was 'THE ONE THAT GOT AWAY'. They were mirror images… He definitely had a type. How on earth did I manage to get his attention? Maybe it was simply the fact that I had served it up on a plate, and he just couldn't resist! Next, there is a different article catches my eye, this was from Jodie herself. All those years ago, I don't think she had ever sold her story, so I was a little shocked to see that Jodie had finally spoken out. I wondered what had changed her mind... There was a picture of her, and she was stood at the front of a house, next to a teenage girl, presumably her daughter. The article wasn't really about Frost, or what he did to her. This article, it was all about the years that she had lost with her mother. She briefly mentioned the trial, but only that had focused on how she now understood why her mum hadn't supported her in court. She said how controlling her stepfather had been. She said that as a teenager she was angry with her mother. However, after the birth of her own daughter, and she had made contact, she understood the abuse that her mother had suffered. She herself knew how difficult things could be. She described the mother-daughter bond as unbreakable... "He may be dead, but he is still in control, and he is the sole reason why my mum and I are not together." I read this phrase over and over, and I wasn't sure if it was the shame that I felt for what I had done to Jodie and her mother, or the medication in my system, but I was immediately sick.

DS Rachel Cooper

Kevin rang, and he had started the telephone conversation by informing me that he had just been "called". On hearing this, my heart was immediately in my mouth, but as I anxiously listened to more of what he had to say... it wasn't that he had called to bollock me for having spoken to Josephine, no, it was quite the opposite. John, had apparently decided to drop the complaint. He said that it was clearly an error of judgment on my part, and he had seen no reason for the Force to lose a good copper over it. Blimey, I didn't expect that!

Kevin, was also extremely apologetic for having accused me of leaking the information to the press. He said that he was angry with me, and it was wrong of him to have jumped to conclusions. Apparently, it was Debbie all along... She had been loose-lipped. She had been at her hair appointment, and had been chatting away to her hairdresser. She had told them everything, and unfortunately for her, rather than this being the type of confessional, where if the seal is broken, you are excommunicated… The hairdresser had disregarded her unwritten oath, and had sold the story for £300! Debbie had only found out when she had gone back in for her roots to be done, and she had been asked for "any more goss?!" Debs was mortified. Although she liked to chat, thankfully, she was also very honest. She went straight to Kevin and told him of her mistake. She had it written up on her record, but luckily for her, that was it, she was keeping her job!

So now that we know how the story got leaked, and that John has decided to let me off, I am free to return to work. Kev told me that they had all but wrapped up the Rosie Flood case, but it was likely that I would still receive a commendation due to my initial groundwork in identifying the suspect, and where the bodies were hidden. I was instrumental in finally giving closure to two victims and their families.

I asked him if my suspension would show up on my record, but apparently, he had yet to do anything official with it, as he had been too busy with the case... It was like it had never happened.... "So, I am pleased to be welcoming you back..."

"Well, actually Gov, can we hold off on that for a couple of weeks?" On hearing my response, his voice was immediately concerned...

"Did you hear what I said? You can come back. Crack some cases. Do what you are good at!"

"Yes, I got all that, but I have a broken toe and it's bloody painful..."

"Oh right.... How on earth did you do that?"

"Um, long story..." I lie. I can't really be telling him that I had had a tantrum because he'd cut me off, so I had kicked out at a wall... After all, how would that look?

"Look, there is nothing pressing. Take two weeks as sick leave, and we'll revisit your situation after then? OK?"

"Ok, thanks Guv." …. And then he was gone… I only had my bloody job back and by the sounds of it, a commendation too… The tide had finally turned!

Josephine

All night I tossed and turned. I couldn't work out if it was the chemo, or what I had read. I had never thought that Jodie might have actually wanted a relationship with her mother. My view had always been monochrome. She had not supported her daughter in court, and therefore she was just as guilty as he was. Simple!

However, what if I had been wrong? What if I'd made a terrible mistake?

Shelley

Today Mum came over for a visit, but I really don't think that she should have done. She looked awful. She's still got her hair, but she's lost more weight and her skin looked grey... She had wanted to spend some quality time with her family. She was tired, having had a rough night. She has a lot on her mind apparently. I know how she feels, I can't seem to sleep these days either...

Anyway, the girls were all over her, and she revelled in their hugs. It was so lovely to see. Understandably she didn't have much of an appetite, and she ate none of the omelette that I had done for her (the only French meal, that I have actually perfected!) She just pushed it around her plate, and she didn't even bother staying for tea. She was worn out. I really hope this chemo is working. I don't know what I'd do if I lost her again!

Shelley

It was lovely, Mum and Dad finally came over... It seems an age since we had had a proper catch-up, and Mum had looked so different. She had lost weight. She attributes it to Slimming World. "Your dad and I are just trying to be a bit healthier that's all, and the meals are quite nice. You should try it!" She said this to me in her sales pitch... I'm sure she's on commission! They both asked after Josephine. Mum had said that she knew exactly what she was going through... I had forgotten that Mum had had Breast Cancer when I was a kid, so of course, she knew all about chemo and the various blood tests and scans. Mum, luckily had been in remission for years...

It was lovely chatting. We didn't do much, just ate lunch and then relaxed in the lounge. The girls were busy playing dress-up, and even put on a show. They were so entertaining. I had forgotten how infectious my mum's laugh was. She was in fits as Heidi was giving out her ludicrous stage directions to Maggie. Even Dad raised a smile. He had been so very serious of late. I hope he is ok. He was definitely worried about something.

Josephine

On my third treatment, I took Shelley with me, and we went for coffee whilst I waited for my bloods to come back. This time I studied the barista intensely to make sure that I was definitely given a decaf. It had been lovely having some time together, but as we left the comfort of the sofas in the Café and I went back up for my treatment, I told her not to stay...

"Are you sure Mum? I really don't mind..."

"No, you get off. Get whatever you need done. There's no point both of us being confined in here."

"Look, I'll come back later to pick you up... I might actually nip home for a nap, I can't seem to keep my eyes open today. It must be the heat!"

Anyway, there I am sat in the chair with my veins growing ever cold, as I start to feel the drugs being administered. I decide to distract myself by looking at the magazines left on the table next to me. I thought

I'd already read everything, but then I saw 'Chat'. It wasn't really my cup of tea, but then beggars can't be choosers…. On the front was a picture of Kelly Frost. I felt like I was being haunted, just like Scrooge in 'A Christmas Carol'. Who would be next? Jacob Marley? She had done an interview from prison. Obviously, the piece was commissioned, following the discovery of the bodies, and the morbid public interest that inevitably followed. She had said how relieved she had been that Jodie's fate was not the same as both Stacey's and Rosie's…

In the article, she said that she had fallen pregnant when she was just 16 years of age. She described how young and naïve she had been as a new mother. She then catalogued the years of abuse that Eric had inflicted upon her. She disclosed that she had only married him, as she had panicked when Jodie's real Dad (her childhood sweetheart) had suddenly died … She didn't want her (Jodie) to grow up without a male role model. So, when Eric Frost, this older man had promised to look after her, and Jodie (and had even adopted her.) She had settled for the financial security and accepted his draconian ways. "I never knew of the abuse. Yes, Jodie was quiet, but I thought it had been because she had just lost her dad and now, she had a new one… I never knew at the time what that bastard did to her…and years later during the court case… well, by then it was too late. I was too scared to go against him. I'll carry that regret with me until the day I die."

She had had absolutely no idea over what he did to Rosie Flood and Stacey Saunders. She did remember his sudden desire to move out of the area, but she never questioned it. "Whatever he said goes… he wanted to move so we did. It certainly never even crossed my mind, that he was a rapist and a serial killer… He must have been spooked after the police had taken his statement."

Kelly spoke of the relationship with her daughter, and explained how she had missed out on being a mum, a grandma, and more than likely great grandma too. "Someone must know who did this... I have done 30 years in this place, and I'm still not eligible for parole. They want me to accept my crime and show remorse; but how can you show remorse for something that you didn't actually do? How can you hide your joy that the man who controlled you, and raped your daughter is dead? Whoever killed him, they did me a favour, I didn't even need to get my hands dirty!" Her words resonated with me. I understood exactly what she meant. I was pleased with what I had done, I had no remorse, well, not for killing him. I had however begun to feel guilty. I felt sick to my stomach. If I'd known then, what I know now, I would never have let her take the blame... I knew how it felt to be deprived of your daughter, but also reunited. I wanted to do something, but what could I do? To tell the truth, would mean that I would definitely leave Shelley... and I wasn't sure if I could do that!

Josephine

My latest treatment completely floored me. I was actually sick in the car on the way home. Of course, Shelley said it didn't matter, and that I shouldn't worry, but I never wanted to be a burden, and now she would be at home cleaning up the mess that I'd left in her car... I was so embarrassed. I practically crawled up the stairs, and I didn't even bother getting changed out of my soiled clothes for bed. I just didn't care. Again, as I did the previous week, I slept all night and well into the next day. I felt so weak and I had such painful sores in my mouth. I was thirsty but when I drank, all I felt was pain. When I did wake up, all I could think about was her (Kelly). I felt so guilty that she had been locked up for something that I did. In the afternoon of the next day, Shelley had come over to see me. She had made me a chicken stew; it was lovely of her, but I just had no appetite. I saw the disappointment in her face when I said I would try some of it later, but even the thought of it made me gag.

"Mum are you ok? Have they said that this is working?"

"I don't know, I have just got to wait and see …. Shelley love, do you believe in karma?"

"Um, not sure, Mum. Why do you ask?"

"Well, maybe this cancer is just punishment for what I have done…"

"Oh Mum, don't be daft…. It's just cancer. It can happen to anyone."

"Look Mum, you are going to beat this. You'll have your op and you will be back to normal. Look, I can see you are tired. I'll leave you to it" she says this as she kisses me on my forehead and lets herself out.

I have no energy to even see her to the door. All I can manage is to pull the sheet around me, and after a minute or so, I have fallen back off to sleep.

Shelley

John and I are just sitting down to dinner. It's the same chicken stew that I had cooked for Mum. The girls have eaten already. They had burger and chips, and to be honest I wished that I'd done us something different too. Stew seemed to be the wrong type of meal for this time of year. I had wanted something wholesome for Mum. As a kid, if I were ever ill, this is what my mum cooked for me…

"Are you eating that, or just playing with it?"

"I am eating, it's just I don't really fancy it. Maybe it's the weather. I knew I should have done us a salad…"

"Actually, why are we eating stew in the middle of a heatwave?"

"I had made it for Mum, I thought it might make her feel better… Mind you, not that she has tried any…"

"Oh Baby, well she only had her treatment yesterday…"

"I know that…. Do you think it is working?"

"I don't know darling, but I'm sure I read somewhere that it's the build-up of the drugs in your system that works…"

"God, I hope so, I'm now rethinking that probation mucking up, and her being locked up would have been preferable… What if I lose her?"

"Look, you can't be jumping ahead… Let's find out what the doctor says at her next appointment…" John says this whilst he pours me the largest glass of wine that I think I've ever seen. I give up on the stew, and head into the lounge where I flop down on the sofa and exhausted with it all, I fall asleep.

Josephine

After a hellish week, I am back at the hospital. I'm seeing Dr Hail, having had a CT scan and more blood tests. I really do feel like a pincushion. I sit in the waiting room patiently for him to come and collect me...
"Ah, Miss Gilling... How are you feeling? Do you want to come through?"
I look up at him, he has such a comforting voice....
"I would have thought you might have brought your daughter with you?" *He says questioning me...*
"No, I didn't want to worry her unnecessarily..."
"I know, but sometimes it's nice to have someone to share the load with."
"Oh, I'm fine... Anyway, how am I getting on? I take it that you have got my results?" *He takes a deep breath...*
"I have..." *He pauses...* "and I wish it was better news... but the tumour doesn't seem to have shrunk any..."

"But I feel rotten, surely it has done something? Are you still going to operate?"

"To be honest, I can't really recommend it. We would be removing so much of the tumour, that there wouldn't be much of you left…" He then told me that he was giving me a two-week break so that my body could recover, and then we would start all over again. It seemed that he was experimenting with my treatment… Usually, it would be a cycle every three weeks, but he was trialling me with a different approach…. Either way, experimental or not, if the tumour wasn't shrinking and he couldn't operate … all of this was only to buy me a little more time… The five-year best-case scenario that he had initially mentioned, seemed completely unobtainable. I felt like I'd been hit with a sledgehammer.

Shelley

After a week away from treatment, Mum seems to be feeling so much better. She has been given some medication to help with the side effects, and today I actually saw her eat something. I almost cried... Maybe things are moving in the right direction for her... I truly hope so... We might get back to France after all.

DS Rachel Cooper

So, I'm back in the office. I took my two weeks and I am glad that I did... My toe although still a little bruised, it no longer throbs and I have actually managed to drive myself in. *Thank the Lord for automatics!* I have also started going through the Frost Case-File, just to catch up on what I have missed. Obviously, the CPS wouldn't be prosecuting him, but I still wanted to be abreast of the evidence. It was tragic to think of what those little girls went through. I felt for the parents of Rosie and Stacey. I know that they now had closure, but it would never heal their pain...

Josephine

I had made my decision. I wanted to see Jodie for myself. The press always liked to present a bias. I needed to make my own assessment. I had decided that today I was going to start my research. I was feeling so much better, not fit like I was before, but at least I was out of bed. I turned on my laptop and put her name into Google. The search results were a plethora of articles, all from different news platforms, but each one of them regurgitating the exact same information. None were of any help in identifying where she lived now. I had already learnt that she had left Essex, soon after her mother had been convicted. I had tried the voters' register, (my remote login at the library luckily still worked) but it was of no use. She clearly wasn't registered to vote. Undeterred, I carried on, but this time I looked at Google images, and there it was, as clear as day... As soon as I saw it, I could not believe that I had missed it the first time. It was the picture of her and her daughter stood outside of her address.

In the background, I could make out the front door, and although the street number was blurred out, I immediately recognised the plaque. I knew exactly where she lived, and it was just down the street from where I had lived as a child. It was Helen's old house. Helen, who I used to take cakes and casseroles to. Helen who used to give me mints every time I visited, and Helen who I had used as an alibi, for giving me enough time to cover up one of the murders. I couldn't remember if I had used her for Ferret Face. God, how ironic it would have been, if I had! Anyway, that picture with the ornate front door and plaque in the background was sufficient to tell me that they lived at number 4 Elm Grove. I had been to that address so many times, it was unmistakable.

Shelley

For two weeks, Mum has had a break from the chemo and it has done her the power of good. She hasn't mentioned whether the previous cycle has worked yet, but maybe she is still awaiting the results. Anyway, tomorrow she starts her next set. I had wanted to take her for a proper 'spa day' before she began again, but she said she didn't fancy being faffed with. I understood, I expect that at the moment she just wants to be left alone. She thinks all of this is karma and her punishment. I've looked into it, and I know it's just the drugs talking, but if she mentions it again, I'm going to tell her what Google says…. Karma is not a punishment, it's an awakening!

Josephine

It's the morning of my next cycle and I couldn't sleep. I was so wound up over it. I got up early and started going through the boxes that I had brought back from Shelley's. I'm sure that there were still some bits that were missing, but I couldn't work out what? An old hymn sheet maybe? Anyway, I pulled out the old makeup bag, and I tried the zip. It was firmly stuck... I had gone to hunt for some wax candles in the kitchen to try out Shelley's suggestion, but I didn't have any. Of course, I had binned them when we had moved. There was so much that I had done, that I now regretted.

On looking through the shoebox, I found a picture of Helen and I outside her house. I remember Mum had taken it. Helen had gotten a new car and she had wanted a photo of me, her and it... It was a Maestro, and looked so dated now... a funny shaped thing, but she had loved that car… And just as I remembered it, there in the background was her ornate front door and the plaque… It was the final confirmation that I needed. I knew exactly where to find Jodie.

Josephine

So here we are again, Groundhog Day…… I'm back at the hospital. I see the same receptionist; she gives me that same sympathetic smile. God, I wish she would laugh at me, tell a joke, anything but that look. I have had months of this now, and I'm still no better. I don't know how much more I can take. She knows that my fate is sealed, and to be honest so do I.

John

Three months have finally passed, and I am so bloody excited. I feel like a kid on his birthday. I actually enjoyed the alarm waking me up this morning. I am finally back to work.

Josephine

I wake up sweating. My dreams had become so vivid... I was with my dad. He was stood, just the other side of our garden gate, beckoning me over.... I initially felt comforted knowing that he was waiting for me, but then I smell him, and I see his beady eyes and flash of blond hair. Ferret Face was there too. My heart was pounding. He was laughing and calling me Lizzy, and he was pulling me back... Tormenting me. I knew it was just the medication; my mind playing tricks, but I couldn't shake the feeling that I needed to do something about it. As I lay there, I kept thinking about the precious time that I had spent with Shelley. How lucky, but also how undeserving I am. I had taken Kelly's liberty and I had absolutely no right.

I had now completed three cycles of the treatment, and enough is enough. I had another scan and again the drugs have done absolutely nothing, well other than making me tired, sick, and paranoid. What quality of life is this? I still haven't told Shelley that it is terminal. I knew that I would never be cured, but I thought, I would have had at least five more years. Poor Shelley, she is still expecting me to have this magical operation, and I'll be free of it. Maybe I should have just told her the truth.

Josephine

I'm not sure what I had been waiting for. I had been watching her in between my treatments. She seems so very timid, always looking down and nothing like the strong girl that I had seen in the courtroom, all those years ago. She was brave and fearless… and everything I wished that I had been back then.

Anyway, I haven't got long left. The cancer is killing me. It is not just that, which is making me feel sick either. It's the guilt; and after my latest nightmare, and the visit from my very own Jacob Marley, aka Ferret Face. I know that I have to set the record straight before it is too late.

I have already typed up my prepared statement. I was well versed in the process, having already been there and done it all with Joseph. I had already gotten my t-shirt and I didn't need, nor want a lengthy consultation. All I wanted was for Isaac to read it out in the interview, and to get this over and done with. I need him to work his magic once again, and to ensure that they don't lock me up. What I did, I now know was wrong, but I did it for the right reasons, surely that counts doesn't it? I still believed that I deserved to die with dignity, alongside my family, and not in a cell.

My statement had taken me days to type up, and it was extremely detailed. It not only covered the murder of Frost, but the others too… I thought that if I was going to tell the truth about one, why not the rest; CJ and my mother included. I knew my confession would certainly lead to Kelly Frost's release, which after all was my ultimate goal. I prayed that this act alone, of me giving her back her freedom and her family, would be enough to absolve me. I had thought that the cancer was my punishment, but what if it wasn't? What if that was just the start? Could the afterlife be even worse?

I arrived at Jodie's address at around 11:00 am, and I knocked on the familiar front door. She opened it almost immediately. She was wearing a beautiful floral dress, with just her bare feet…
"Can I help you?" She said in a low hushed tone…. I wasn't really sure what to say…so initially, I began to stutter, as I tried to form some kind of sentence…
"Um… yes… I'm… My name is Josephine Gilling, I have some information that will help your mother's case…"
She looked at me quizzically, but then she asked…
"Are you the press?" She sounded nervous…
"No, no I'm not… look, can I come in?"
"Well, my partner is upstairs. You'll have to be very quiet …"
"Ok, yes, no problem, I can do that…" I say this almost in a whisper.

She invites me in, and as she turns to walk back inside, I notice that she still has the label sticking out at the back of her dress… I'm not sure whether I should tell her… so I don't… just in case it causes any embarrassment. I didn't want to do anything, that might make her change her mind about listening to what I had to say. It was important that I told her the truth… She ushered me into her lounge room. It was all very familiar, although Helen's preference for the popular '70's geometric décor, was clearly long gone!

"So, you said you could help my mum. How do you know her?"
"I don't actually, but…" I really wasn't sure where to start… So, I began by saying that like her, I too had been a victim of sexual abuse. She seemed uncomfortable by this, and started to look down at the floor. I was desperate to keep her attention… I needed her to listen long enough to me, so that I got to the punchline… I told her that no one had believed

me either... and that she had been stronger than I was. She had at least gone to court. "I remember you, all those years ago, and how cruel the Defence Barrister had been.... All of those names they had called you."

"Oh, so you are a journalist? Did you cover the story?"

"No, no, I'm not... I was just an interested party..."

"How do you mean?" ...

"Um... Look, I'm not sure how to tell you this... Maybe it's best to just come out and say it... It wasn't your mum that killed Eric, it was me!"

My heart was racing, but I'm not sure that she had even heard what I had said to her, as at the same time as I had finally confessed, there had been the sound of movement upstairs. This had immediately unsettled her. I hear the heavy thud of footsteps coming down the stairs, and I then see an angry-looking male in the doorway. He is dressed in just a vest and boxers, and I later find out that this heavy-set male is Jodie's partner, Gary.

"Oh, Gary…" *Her voice wobbles,* "Sorry, I really didn't mean to wake you…"

"What's all the noise, Jodie? Who's this?"

"She says that she can help my mum. This is Josephine… Sorry Josephine, you were saying?" She turns back to me, but Gary is clearly unhappy at being so easily dismissed, so he says…

"Have you offered our guest a cup of tea?" Again, she seems nervous in her reply…

"Um, no… sorry! I didn't think… Can I get you one?"

"Oh, no I'm fine, but thank you. I just want to get what I came to tell you out of the way…" Ignoring me, he then says demandingly…

"Well, I want one! Jodie, come on. Kitchen now!"

She looks both flustered and embarrassed, and she tries to make light of his bullish behaviour… "I'm sorry Josephine, I'll be back in a minute. It's just… he can't do anything for himself… I don't think he even knows how to switch the kettle on!" I smile at her as she gets up. He is right behind her now, practically manhandling her towards the rear of the house. "Is that a new dress, Jodie? You silly girl, you seem to have forgotten to remove the label!" He says this, as he pushes her through the opening of the frosted glass door, slamming it behind them. With the force that he used, I was surprised that it didn't shatter. I was left there alone. Sat on the sofa and wondering if she had actually heard what I had said. Then I hear muffled, but clearly raised voices coming through the wall. I then see rapid movement through the glass door, and it looks and sounds like they are having a fight. I go to see what is going on. The last thing that I wanted to do was be the cause of any problems. I was here to right a wrong. I walk through the door...

"Um... Do you need any help with the tea?"

"What are you doing in here? No, she doesn't need any help, and I am in the middle of a private conversation with my Mrs!" Jodie then speaks up. She is crying, and the left side of her face looks red as if it's been hit ... "Gary, it is only a dress..."

"It's a fucking rag, and you have been spending my money again…"

"I didn't. I promise. It was my money from the article…" I'm just stood there not knowing what to do… Then Gary turns to me again… "Why are you still here? Fuck Off!" I then just come out with it…

"I need to tell you… Jodie, I'm so sorry, it wasn't your mum that killed Eric, it was me!"

At the same time as I say this, I see Gary go to swipe Jodie across her face. I then notice the black-handled knife. It is just lying there on the kitchen side. Then before I know what has happened, I feel the blood spatter and I look down as the bright red liquid starts to seep through my clothing. I know that I haven't got much time.

Shelley

It's late morning and my phone begins to ring. I pick it up and it is the hospital. The female voice tells me that my mother has been admitted, and that I need to get there as soon as possible. Her exact words were "You need to come now; she's not got long...". Panicked, I jump straight into the car and race immediately there.... I try to call John on route but he doesn't answer ... Abandoning my car, I run into the Accident and Emergency and straight up to the Reception Desk. My heart is pounding, my head the same...

Out of breath, I say... "I've just been called; my name is Shelley Jones. My mum...." As I was just relaying this, a passing nurse overhears me.

"Was that Shelley Jones, you said? Are you here about your mum?"

"Yes, yes!" My voice is shaking....

"Come with me. She is in a side room." I follow her hurriedly and then she points and says… "She's in there darling…"

John

I am on a tea break and sat in the canteen. We have just had a morning of yelling at each other to "SHOW ME YOUR HANDS…" and "GET BACK!" as we practice our heel palm strikes, and the various other defensive moves… I'm on an 'Officer Safety Training Refresher'. Another tick in the box, for getting me back to being out and about. I had my phone switched off, as per the demands of the militant Instructor, and now that I am swigging down my coffee, I turn it on to see if I've missed anything. I have a text message to tell me that I missed a call from Shelley, and as I'm just about to call her back, an unknown number flashes up.
"Hello"
"Yes, that's right, she's my mother-in-law."
"Ok, thanks for letting me know."
The call terminates. It was the hospital. They had got my number from the emergency contact details, that they had on record... They had already rung Shelley

apparently. I call her to see if she has any news …. She picks up immediately.

"Why didn't you answer? I've been calling you…" I can't tell whether she is angry or frustrated, but her voice sounds strange…

"What's the matter? Look, you've got me now."

"It's Mum…" I cut her off…

"Yes, I know! She didn't turn up for treatment. The hospital has already called me…"

"What? What treatment?"

"Err Josephine, her chemo?!" I say a little sarcastically.

No, I didn't mean Mum, I meant **Mum** Mum, she's…. she's." Shelley seems to struggle with what she's trying to say…

"She's what, Baby?"

"She's dead!" I can't quite work it out…

"What did you say? You mean, Patty?"

"Yes, she had collapsed… I'm at the hospital."

"Ok, I'll come now, give me 20 minutes. OK?"

"OK… John…. What was that you were saying about Mum and the hospital?"

"She hasn't turned up for treatment… Look, let me track her down and make sure that she is alright, then I'll be with you. Ok?"

Shit!

I end the call to Shelley and immediately I call Josephine. It goes straight to voicemail. As time is of the essence, and I need to get to Shelley, I decide to pull up the little tracking app that I had put on her phone. I'd not looked at it for months. I had no reason to. I had absolutely no worries about her potentially reoffending…. It begins to load, and as I wait impatiently for it to show me her location, there is a mass exodus of officers from the canteen. It's nothing unusual for them to leave their refs half-eaten. Rushing out to deal with the next emergency call. One officer still remains. She has her wrist bandaged, so clearly, she is on light duties… I turn to her

"What was that about?"

"Stabbing, I think? I'm just listening to the channel now… units are already there. They just wanted backup…"

"Ah, OK."

I turn back to my task and I finally have a pin in the map…. It's not an address that I recognise, 4 Elm Grove. I decide to go there en route to the hospital, just to check in on her. As I get up to leave, I can hear the radio chatter. An officer on scene is speaking to control, and he is requesting a van and space for one…

"Sorry 674, just to clarify, can you confirm location and what it is for?"

"Yes, control. 4 Elm Grove, and it's for murder."

Shelley

I still couldn't take it all in! I had rushed in expecting to see my mum.... and it was my mum that was lying there, with the white sheets pulled up around her... but it didn't make any sense. It wasn't Josephine in that bed. It was my adoptive mother! My mum, who had taken care of me as a child, wiped away all of my tears, and loved me as her own. It was the Mum who hadn't been attending the hospital every week for treatment. It was the Mum that wasn't sick! I went to grab her hands and try to comfort her. I wanted to tell her that I was there. It was only then that it began to dawn on me, for her usually warm hands were cool.... I think I had already realised, but my worst fears were then confirmed. There was a comforting hand on my shoulder, and then a voice which said... "I'm so sorry darling, they should have said... she's already gone."

My mum had died and I hadn't been there. I didn't know why she was even at the hospital. My dad, who was usually my mum's shadow, was nowhere to be seen, and for the first time in a long while, I felt completely and utterly alone.

John

FUCK!!!! My head is bloody pounding! I look at the map that is displayed on my phone, and then where the pin is. I then carefully read the address again. 4 Elm Grove...

"Sorry Mate, what address did they just say?" Immediately she replies with...

"4 Elm Grove. Why? Do you know it?"

"Um... No, just curious..." I try to sound calm, but inside I am anything but... I had not even considered that she would kill again... She was fucking ill! For goodness' sake! What was it? One for the road?

I was torn... what do I do? Go to Shelley who is with her mother, lying dead in the hospital, or do I go to see if I can help sort out, whatever mess that Josephine has gotten herself into now? I tried calling Shelley, but the phone wouldn't connect. So, I did the only thing that I knew I must do... I went to the hospital to comfort my wife… Fuck you, Josephine! You have made your bed and you can bloody well lie in it!

Shelley

I have finally found my dad. He had gone outside to get some air... He was busy cursing my mum, calling her stubborn...

"Dad, are you ok?"

"No, not really. You know your mother is dead, do you?" His words seemed uncharacteristically harsh. He was understandably very upset...

"What happened?"

"What do you mean?"

"Well, what happened to Mum?"

"Well, I suppose now, I can tell you, seeing as she is not here anymore to stop me. She had secondary breast cancer... She's been having treatment ..." I interrupt him...

"What? When did all this happen?"

"It was just before you all decided to bugger off to France. I told her to tell you but she wouldn't. She didn't want you to change your plans..."

"But I wouldn't have gone..."

"Exactly! Anyway, our "holidays" in Cornwall was her having treatment..."

"But why didn't she tell me once I was back home?"

"Oh, you know your mum, she knew how worried you were about Josephine... She didn't want to load you... and make your anxiety come back... you had been so happy..."

"But Dad... I deserved to know; I would have spent more time with her... Oh my god, what am I going to tell the girls?" I well up at the thought.

"Dad... what happened this morning... they said she had collapsed?"

"Yes, just that.... This morning she collapsed... and I brought her straight here. They think it was some sort of clot on her lung... Is she still in the room? Look, I have got to go back. I should never have left her; I was just so angry..." We go back inside, and down the corridor... The nurse is in the room with Mum. She is busy writing something up... Just then my phone rings... it's John.

John

I called Shelley from the Hospital Carpark as I was on my way towards the main reception area. She answered straight away. I still wasn't sure if I should tell her about Josephine, but I needed to see firstly how fragile she was after Patty. It had been a massive shock...

"Hi Baby, where are you?"
"We are still in A&E; Mum is in a side room. Look, come to the reception area of the Accident and Emergency and I'll meet you there..."
"Ok... See you in a minute..." I walk purposefully into the building, and immediately I spot her... Her mascara has run, she has clearly been crying. She seems for now, however, and rather unexpectedly to be quite composed...
I go straight over to her and I hug her... "I'm so, so sorry..." She nuzzles her head into me, and I can

physically feel her crumble... "John, she had cancer. She never said... She was trying to protect me..."

"Oh, Baby..." I don't really know what to say, so I hug her tightly, to try and take away her pain... "Where is she now?"

"Dad is with her..."

"He had gone off, but I found him outside. He needed some air... Actually.... talking about finding people... Did you find my mum?" I was dreading this question... "Umm... yes I did. I know exactly where she is, and she's safe... Anyway, shall we go and see your dad? I expect he needs our support." I say this with the hope of changing the conversation before she asks anything further about Josephine.

I follow Shelley towards a side room, and there from the doorway, I see Colin. He was sat down at Patty's bedside; it was heart-breaking to see. He was kissing her now cold hands and face, and telling her how much he loved her... The Nurse came up to us...

"I'm so sorry for your loss…. Um… The Porter will be taking her soon. Do you want to take her jewellery? I did speak to Dad, but I think it's all too much for him."
"Ok." I say, speaking for both of us… "Yes, that's fine. We can sort that out…"
Shelley and I both go into the little room… I go over to Colin and I shake his hand. "I'm so sorry…" As I say this, he looks up at me, and I see tears cascading down his grief-stricken face.

Josephine – 30 minutes earlier.

I watch as he falls to the floor, hitting his head on the work surface as he does. I recognise this scene, and I know that without even checking his pulse, that Gary is dead….

She is just stood there. She looks at me, and then at him. The knife too has fallen, landing next to his lifeless body and a pool of his blood. I had to act quickly… I picked up the knife and I wiped it clean. She was watching me do this and still not saying a word. Her mouth just hung open.
"Right, we haven't got long… take off your dress…"
She looked at me quizzically… and I repeat my instruction… "Take off your dress!"
"Look… you take mine…" I pass mine over, having already taken it off, and I'm stood there, just in my knickers and bra… Thankfully we were practically the same size… She, after initially hesitating does as I ask

and removes hers too. I can see that her whole body is covered in bruises, some yellow, some purple…

"Oh, my goodness… did he do this?" She doesn't say anything, she just continues to look directly at me…
"Right, I'm going to call an ambulance… Where is your house phone?"
"But isn't he dead?" These are the first words that she has said…
"Yes, but we need some time… Look I'm going to make the call, and if you can manage it, see if you can sound hysterical in the background…" She looks confused… but I have a plan… Anyway, having seen the phone on the kitchen surface…. I dial 999. The operator immediately asks what service I require…
"Ambulance please, he has been stabbed! Oh yes, the address 4 Elm Avenue… Please come quickly." I end the call… and it immediately starts ringing… I don't answer. She was silent. No hysterical cries as I had

asked. She looks at me and then she says, very matter of fact...

"You gave them the wrong address..."

"Yes, I know!" I then begin calmly to explain to her what is about to happen...

"Jodie, please listen to me... They are going to call the police, and they will arrive with the ambulance crew. I know this because I have seen enough of those police documentaries on the TV, to know their protocol. But I also know that they are not coming straight here. They are going to Elm Avenue... Please, just sit on the floor and listen to me. I need you to understand why I am here.... Right, you have a daughter, yes?" She slides down the kitchen surface, and to the floor. She is clearly in shock...

"Yes, Maxine..."

"And how old is Maxine?" She starts to sob...

"17..."

"Was that the age that you were, when your mum went to prison?"

"Almost. I was 18, but what's that got to do with anything?" I don't answer her...

"Look… at any minute, they are going to be arriving at Elm Avenue, and they are going to realise that it's the wrong address… They will then check the origin of the phone call and realise that it's here…"

The house phone continues to keep ringing in the background…

"That is them now, still trying to get hold of me… So, listen and listen good. I'm not sure if you actually heard me before, but I came here today to tell you that it was me who had killed Eric, and not your mum…" She is looking at me, but remains silent…
"I attended your court case all those years ago and I was disgusted by his and your mother's actions. I could not believe it when he was acquitted, so I decided to get justice for you. I killed him and I disposed of his body. I then kept quiet when your

mother was linked to the murder and convicted. I didn't do this just to save my own skin. It's just, I felt that she was equally to blame for the abuse that you had suffered…" She starts to speak and tries to defend her mother. I cut her off, I don't have the time.

"Look, I know that you want to stick up for her, but I need you to listen to me… I was wrong… I did not understand that she was a victim herself… Were the papers right about what he did to her?" She nods… "Anyway… I am dying and I can't do that, if I know that your mum is still locked up for a crime that she didn't do… So, I came here to tell you that I'm sorry, and that I am going to go to the police…"

I can hear sirens. They are coming, and I know that at any minute, I am going to be arrested…

"You tell them the truth that I came here to confess to your stepdad's murder. You tell them that Gary had gone to hit you, and I grabbed a knife and I stabbed him… You tell them nothing else, and that the rest is a blur… OK."

She goes to open her mouth to speak, but then she stops as she is startled by the *"BANG, BANG, BANG"* on the front door… The cavalry has arrived. I pick up the knife…

The heavy knock was enough to announce their presence, but as I walk over to open the door, I can also see the blue flashing lights illuminating the bay front window. As I open the door, a tall male officer begins to speak…

"We've been called to the report of a stab…" He doesn't finish his sentence as he clocks my bloody dress and the knife in my hand…
"PUT THE KNIFE DOWN!" He shouts this, and then he takes a step back… Immediately I do as he commands and I say… "I killed him…"

Josephine

It all seemed to happen so fast... I was taken to one side, and then in rushed the ambulance crew and another officer... I could hear Jodie in the background sobbing uncontrollably. There was a little toing and froing from the kitchen, and then the other officer (who was with the paramedics) confirmed that he was dead. I was then arrested and cautioned for Gary's murder, and handcuffed to the rear... It had reminded me of when John had transported me in the back of his car, when I had flown back from Dubai... it's not a comfortable place to have your hands... I was then searched... I heard the male officer's radio chirp...
"Officers at Elm Grove receiving? ...Your carriage awaits..."
"Yep received..."
"Right, that's us... Come with me..." I hadn't yet said anything further to him. No reply to caution, nothing. I wanted to save it all for the Custody Suite, and get everything documented properly. I didn't want to

have to repeat my story… He has a firm grip on my arm, as we are about to step through the front door, and out towards the light show ahead… I've never seen anything like it… so many police cars, the van, the ambulance, and every one of them with their lights flashing… I then, suddenly realise that I haven't got my statement, and we are about to leave… I urgently shout!

"Wait! My bag! I need my bag!" He stops, but he doesn't release his strong hold on my arm…

"Is it this one?" He says whilst pointing over to my brown leather tote, which is still at the side of the sofa…

"Yes, that's the one… It's very important. You must not lose it!"

"Okey Dokey, let's go…" I am then walked out into the fresh air, and helped up into the rear of the police van. It's actually got a cage… It's like the ones that I had seen on the TV… You see, that the last time that I was arrested, I had had none of this drama.... This time it was actually quite exciting...

"Has she been searched, Mate?" I hear the driver ask the tall officer this. The one who had arrested me...

"Yes, Mate... I'm not one of your probies. I know what I'm doing..."

"Ok, are you coming with us, or do you want Jess in the back with her?"

"I'll come... The HAT (*Homicide Assessment Team*) will be all over this place soon... And I just want to get her booked in, a skeleton report put on, and my notes done... They will be barking their orders soon enough..."

"Yep, I hear you..."

The cage had already been shut behind me, but then I feel a sudden rush of air, as they slam the rear doors too. The air inside the van in comparison now feels flat, and there is a brief silence. It is peaceful. I then hear a scrape, as the arresting officer slides open the van's middle doors. He climbs in and then sits on the lone seat opposite me, on the other side of a Perspex screen. He is expressionless.

"Are we good to go?" Shouts the driver from the front.

"Yep... let's get to the Nick... I've got tickets for a gig tonight, and this was the last thing that I bloody needed..."

Josephine

I was escorted into the Custody Area, and I was immediately greeted by the same grey-haired Sergeant from before. He looks over his glasses at me...

"Well, I honestly never expected to see you in here again…. Shall we get you booked in?"

"Come on, let's have it… What's she been up to?" The officer that arrested me, seemed to reel everything off super quickly… He was in such a hurry… Reason, time of arrest, etc… I had definitely made the right call to stay silent till now… What if he'd missed something important?

"Was there any reply to caution?" The Sergeant directs this to the PC who is stood at the side of me, clearly wishing that he wasn't!

"Nope, she's not said anything. Well, apart from when she opened the door to me, and so this was before I had cautioned her. She said, "I killed him!" She still had the knife in her hand!"

"Righty-ho... Has she signed that in your scene notes?"

"No. Notes have been delayed, due to securing of the prisoner... It's all on this..." He says tapping this square box on his chest... *Of course! They wear cameras!*

"Ok Josephine... Did you say that?"

"Yes, I did. I stabbed him and now he is dead..." I can feel a slight irritation in right eye itch, as I say this quite convivially... but I didn't just stop there... I was getting everything off my chest!

"Sergeant, I also need to be further arrested for the murders of Paul Briggs, Eric Frost, Geraint Pike, my own mother Nancy Gilling, and Charlie Jacobs..."

"Well, I wasn't expecting that!" ... The Sergeant says this sounding surprised! "Do the honours will you?" I hear the chap who arrested me swear under his breath... "Well, I'm definitely not making that fucking gig now!"

"Sorry, did you say something?"

"No Sarge…." The PC, then reluctantly further arrests and cautions me for all of the other murders... My reply to caution was simply to inform them that my prepared statement, as well as the murder weapon (my dad's knife) for the stabbings of Briggs, Frost, and Pike, was in the makeup bag wrapped up in my dad's old hanky…. "See I told you that my bag was important!... Oh yes, I also need to apologise. The zip on the makeup bag is stuck. My granddaughter, she accidentally broke it, so you'll have to cut it open to get the knife out. So be careful …" I really didn't want anyone getting hurt…

The Sergeant took it all down, but I could see the disbelief in his face… I suppose that this wasn't a run of the mill thing to happen! "You also might want to let DS Cooper know that I'm here too… I expect she'll be quite interested…"

"Well! That was some reply to caution!" The Sergeant finishes off the booking in process, and he then asks if I need any legal representation? I immediately ask for Isaac Brown... Not that I really needed his assistance with the interview, but I wanted to explain myself to him. I also still hoped that he would manage to sort out bail.

"Have you got any medical issues; do you need to see the nurse?" The Sergeant asks me this whilst checking on my welfare... I obviously said nothing about the cancer.... I would only inform them once I was charged. I was searched by a female officer, and then a tall ginger lad was called over to process me... I smiled for the camera and gave them my prints. ... They even did me a manicure, retaining my fingernail clippings. Then they gave me a rather comfy tracksuit, as they had wanted my dress as evidence. I felt like I was in my favourite pyjamas! Handy really, as I was completely exhausted!

The day had been rather more eventful than I could have imagined... So, when I was told that I was now going to be put into my cell, I was actually relieved.

"Do you want a blanket?" The ginger gaoler asked me, just before closing the wicket…

"Actually yes, if you don't mind, and a cup of water…"

The room service had definitely improved since my last visit!

I couldn't describe to you how I felt stood up at the desk. For years I had carried with me what I had done. I still didn't feel remorse as such, but by telling the truth, the weight had been lifted and I was finally free.

DS Rachel Cooper

Oh, my actual fucking god!!!! I was right. I was bloody right... You couldn't write this stuff and even if you did, no one would believe you... Anyway, downstairs in the cells is my nemesis, Josephine Gilling.... The one that got away... Well, she is not going to this time! I am going to make sure of it! Not only has she killed again, which I suspected that she might, but she has also now confessed to the murders of Paul Briggs, Eric Frost, and Geraint Pike... My cold cases; and even to her own mother's murder!? Well, I never suspected that one ... She's also confessed to slaughtering her rapist; Charlie Jacobs! She is a SERIAL KILLER!! I feel like shouting it from the rooftops that I WAS RIGHT!!!

Right now, however, I am trying to negotiate with the SIO (Senior Investigating Officer) on the Gary Wilkinson case, her latest victim. I have requested that he lets me take the lead…. I have already spoken to Kevin and he said I probably do deserve to run with this, but if you looked at it objectively, she is a serial killer of 7 victims… and it is very likely to become a high-profile case. "Think about it, it was only really months since she was given a suspended sentence and allowed to roam free… It is going to turn that landmark ruling on its head… The press is going to have a field day." I fully understood what he was saying, but I was so desperate to get into that interview room with her. I finally wanted to get my confession and charge.

John

We had just got home from the hospital; Colin, Shelley, and myself. I had left my car up there, and I planned to collect it later as I didn't think I should let Shelley's dad drive. I had half expected to be doing two runs back up there to collect Shelley's too, but she actually seemed quite together... Anyway, the kettle is on to make them both a sweet cup of tea, before collecting the girls from Jeanette's... It should have been Josephine doing the grandma duties, but God only knows what she's been up to. I thought she was sick!

My phone rings. I see Rachel's name flash up on the screen. I know exactly why she is calling, but I try my very best to sound surprised as I answer...

"Oh Rachel, I wasn't expecting you to call... have you been doing any illegal searches recently?" She ignores this, clearly very confident in what she is about to tell me... Her assertive tone confirms what I had already suspected...

"Hi John, I was just calling out of courtesy" ... *to gloat she means*... "I wanted to advise you that we have Josephine with us in custody at the moment. She has just killed a man, and has also confessed to the murders of another five, including those cold cases!" Her voice sounds questioning... I know she wants to know if I knew... I had really fucked up... Anyway, I respond by saying "Oh OK" and I try not to show any shock or emotion. "Well thank you for letting me know, but we've had a family bereavement, so I'll have to catch up with you another day. Thank you for your call." I don't even let her respond. I just press the end call button.

"Who was that?" Shelley immediately asks me.
"It was Rachel..."

"Rachel? Rachel, as in DS Cooper?" She says this clearly annoyed.

"What does she want?"

"Nothing darling. Well, nothing important" … I wasn't sure if I should be keeping this from her, but I truly felt that tonight should be all about Patty.

DS Rachel Cooper

I called John to let him know that we had Josephine in custody, but he was really strange. It was as if he already knew... He said something about a bereavement and then he hung up on me... What bereavement? ... Maybe he had meant the death of his career? He's got to have known! Anyway, I have been told that I am <u>not</u> to be the Lead Investigator. The HAT wasn't going to step away. However, they had said that I could ride shotgun, and DI Griggs was on his way here for us to talk strategy. Isaac Brown was also on route. We might just get this all wrapped up tonight. She would be put before the court tomorrow morning, and this time I would make sure that she would be going to prison...

Central Custody

Clearly, someone somewhere had said the Q word, as late turn had suddenly got busy! Only a few cells were left, and the radio had been non-stop. Officers constantly calling up and securing a space for their prisoner. Soon it will be shut. Declared as full... and no one ever willingly wants to go off borough. Police Officers very much prefer being dealt with by their own team... There is nothing more frustrating than going to another borough, or even worse another force... The queuing system then goes completely out of the window, as nepotism becomes the deciding factor in who gets dealt with first...

Anyway, Bob Smythe is the late turn skipper and he is taking his sweet time booking in the prisoners, and then signing them back into custody after interview, etc ... There is already a queue of three other prisoners waiting at the back gate to come in... and more on their way...

"Right, I'm having a tea break..."
"Sorry, Sarge could you just add this interview tape to the record before you go?" Says a young DC who has been waiting patiently, and failing miserably to attract his attention...
"Actually, no I can't. You'll have to wait until after my break... just like everyone else..."
She knows that she just has to take it, and stand there another 20 minutes, and wait for the fat middle-aged sergeant to finish his cuppa, and dunked digestive before he will do the 30-second job of adding the interview tape serial number to the custody record! .... He really is a git!

All of a sudden... just as Bob has got up on to his feet to switch on the kettle; Billy, one of the gaolers comes sprinting up to the desk...

"Sarge...sarge!" *He is out of breath and clearly panicking...*

"What is it, Billy?" Sergeant Smythe says, overtly annoyed at being interrupted on his break...

"It's number 12... She's not breathing!"

"What?" *A little panicked*.... The Sergeant then very uncharacteristically abandons his tea break, and runs after Billy and down to the cells. On the way past, he hollers at the Custody Nurse who is partway through her examination of another detainee....

"Leave that one, number 12... isn't breathing!"

Straight away, Smythe is in the cell, having turned the unresponsive and sallow-faced prisoner onto her back. He immediately starts CPR ... He barks at Billy to call for an ambulance, and after what feels like forever, the Custody Nurse eventually makes an appearance ...

"What have we got here?" She says in a very calm and nonchalant manner...

"I'm not sure to be honest... There was nothing in the handover notes..."

She comes closer to the detainee and Bob. He immediately stops his task of 30 chest compressions to 2 breaths… Billy now has also come along with the defibrillator… Bob is expecting her to take over, but she doesn't. She simply looks up at both of them and states in a very matter of fact way. "You are wasting your time there… She is long gone…. She is dead!"

Sergeant Smythe had already thought that she might have been, but he'd hoped as he had foolishly checked her airway, blown-in those few rescue breaths, and pumped her chest ironically in time to the Bee Gee's hit of 'Staying Alive', that he was wrong… No one ever wants to be connected to a death in Police Custody, and certainly not to be the one who is ultimately responsible for their care!

DS Rachel Cooper

There I am rather impatiently waiting for DI Griggs to arrive. I have all of the files out for the historical cases and I'm ready to go…. Suddenly the desk phone rings… There is a male DC also in the office, but he just looks at it… "I'll get it shall I?" I say picking it up… "It won't bloody bite!" Anyway, it turns out to be Custody for me. I recognise Billy's voice… I instantly think that Smythe has got him to chase me up and ask what the delay is… I was all ready to tell them that this was a HAT job, and that I was just tagging along for the ride, when he says… "It's your prisoner, Josephine Gilling…. She is dead!"

EPILOGUE

DI Rachel Cooper

It was certainly not what I was expecting. I had been really looking forward to staring my nemesis directly in the eyes, and getting a confession. I had hated that she had played me for a fool. She had nearly lost me my bloody job, and I was going to enjoy nailing her to the mast!

Anyway, after she had very inconveniently died (denying me of that pleasure). DI Gregg also did a backpedal. Once he knew that he would no longer be taking down a serial killer, and there would be no career-enhancing high-profile trial. He was all too keen to pass the full investigation over to me, including her latest victim of Gary Wilkinson…. He was the long-term partner of Jodie Frost, and by all accounts, a real nasty bastard. He had abused her for years. We had been called to that address so many times… Although not that it achieved anything. Jodie would never provide a statement, or have any photos taken of her injuries, and as the 999 calls were only ever from concerned neighbours, and not from Jodie herself - there was never the chance of any background noise to prove what he had done to her. She just seemed to take it! We had tried for numerous victimless prosecutions, but the CPS just weren't willing to run with it. He had gotten away with it for years, well not anymore!

My first puzzle to solve, was why Josephine would have even been at that address? However, after I had read the initial account that the attending officers had obtained, and then I had Jodie in, to take her statement, it all started to make sense.
Eric Frost was one of my cold case victims, and he was Jodie's stepfather. There was a court case where he was accused of sexually abusing her as a child in the late 1970's to early '80's. This court case is where Josephine had first gotten to know about the abuse.

The court had acquitted Eric, and Josephine being Josephine had decided that she would bring her own form of justice (the terminal type...)

Jodie had apparently been just six-years-old when the abuse began, the very same age as both Rosie and Stacey. I had come across an image of Jodie at that time, and it was uncanny how alike she had been to those missing two girls... It was unsettling to know that she might have had a very different fate, if he hadn't been married to her mother! I wondered if that was what had stopped him from killing her too? Anyhow, Josephine murdering Eric Frost, meant that Jodie's justice came at a very high price. She had also lost her mother not long afterwards, as she was wrongly convicted of his murder. Someone had provided an eye-witness statement at the time, putting Kelly wrongly in the frame... I said it all along that Josephine and Kelly looked alike. See! I wasn't obsessed!

Kelly Frost had said she was innocent all along... Although they all say that... If I had a pound for everytime I heard that, I'd be in the Bahamas by now and not sitting in a dusty office surrounded by case-files, and the station mice for company!! Unbelievably she was actually telling the truth! That poor woman; she has spent the last 30 years locked up for a crime that she didn't commit...

Anyway, up until recently none of this seemed to worry our Josephine. She had always thought the mother was complicit in Eric's crime, and therefore considered her equally to blame... (She very helpfully explained all of this in her very detailed prepared statement... It outlined every part of her thought process, and resultant action that she took). Well, that was of course, before she had gotten to know her own daughter, and realised how sacred the mother-daughter bond is, and probably more importantly before I had started digging into the Rosie Flood case... It was after the story broke of what Eric had been up to; and that the papers had uncovered, and reported details on the Frost's abusive marriage. Only then, had Josephine realised her mistake. The magazine article where Jodie had said that she really missed her mum and had forgiven her, it had been instrumental in helping to change Josephine's attitude.

Anyway, on that day, Josephine has turned up at the address of Jodie Frost. She had the clear intention of going there to tell Jodie what she had done. She must have been planning to hand herself into the police straight afterwards, as she had had the prepared statement already in her handbag, along with the murder weapon... I still cannot believe that this was not found in the original house search... If it had been, we would never have had this situation where she was free to kill again.

Jodie was really rather vague in relation to how Gary got stabbed, and she puts this down to PTSD. She thinks that she has buried the memories... (Now where have I heard that one before?!!) Josephine had started to tell Jodie as to why she was at her address.... Gary, then on hearing voices, is woken up... He comes down the stairs and orders Jodie into the kitchen... and he starts shouting at her, and they begin arguing .... Jodie then says what happened next was all a blur. All she can remember is seeing Josephine in the kitchen. She sees the knife and then Gary is on the floor... dead! I was initially suspicious of her story. She had seemed very nervous in telling it to me, and there were elements that seemed to have too much detail, and others where there was simply not enough... even his post-mortem report showed that the stab wound positioning appeared more in keeping with self-defence. However, she had not mentioned anything about him trying to strike Josephine at the time, nor in her statement; PTSD or not... I had already sent Josephine's clothing off for analysis, and as we all know, the science doesn't lie….and sure enough the blood spatter evidence was conclusive. She had been the one to stab him, no doubt! … Anyway, Jodie lost her partner that day, which (from a non-policing perspective) might not actually be a bad thing.

I still can't work out Josephine's motive, there was nothing to suggest that he had ever sexually abused anyone, and unfortunately for me, she had inconveniently died, before I could ask her the question … Anyway, Jodie will soon be reunited with her mother after 30 years apart, as I have just finished the paperwork to get her conviction overturned. Every cloud as they say!

The knife in the makeup bag was like the magic key. It unlocked all of them… matching not only the striation marks on what was left of the bodies, but also having the DNA of Paul Briggs, Eric Frost, and Geraint Pike. I did inform the families about their loved ones, and I let them know, that we had finally discovered who was responsible, but none of them seemed to care. Briggs's ex-wife had remarried and didn't want to know, and nor did her son. He had changed his name by deed poll, as he wanted no association with his dead paedophile father. Pike's only living relative was his brother, and once I had answered his query in the negative, as to whether he would be getting any financial compensation for the years of not knowing what had happened. He too couldn't have cared less as to who was responsible for his brother's demise. As for Josephine's mother, there was no one to inform of how she had passed. However, from reading Josephine's confession, whereby she detailed the deliberate overdosing of her mother with the prescribed morphine. This appeared to have been done with love and mercy in mind. I had obviously requested her medical records from the time, and the GP had recorded that she hadn't got long left anyway... Although still wrong, her murder was very different... there was no hint of revenge. This was a very different case to when she had finally caught up with her own childhood rapist in Dubai. I'm not sure why, but she didn't provide any details of his demise... not like in all of the others. In those, she had explained each of their interactions, and what her rationale was for taking their life. For Jacobs, however, she simply stated that she had arranged to meet him and she had put a dagger through his heart. I had already read the Police Report (translated of course) from the Dubai Officers, so I already knew this. So, with nothing else to share with them, I simply provided an exhibited copy of her statement. They of course, were delighted as like here, it is always great to gain closure on a case.

The only thing in all of this that had confused me initially, was why now? And this was only answered after having received her Post Mortem Examination Report. It was then immediately apparent. She was riddled with cancer, and had had a predicted life expectancy of only a few months. She wasn't really taking a gamble in confessing; she was simply putting all of her affairs in order. Her internet history had confirmed this, as some weeks previous, she had searched for cases where the accused were discharged, having been deemed too sick to stand trial… She had simply wanted to confess to her sins. She had already been given a death sentence.

I suppose I have to be grateful to her in a way… Things all seem to have turned out for the better…. Sergeant Bob Smythe has turned over a new leaf. Her dying on his watch seems to have humbled him, and he is actually being helpful… It's surprising how many friends you realise that you need when you're the subject of an IOPC Investigation!

As for me... Well, I am now a newly promoted Detective Inspector, and I have just got back from a Commendation Ceremony.... And that is not all.... I am also just about to go out for a celebratory meal with my boyfriend!

Yes, believe it or not, after it had all come out that she had been responsible for my cold case murders. I had bumped into Stu in the corridor. I had still felt so bad for having mucked everything up so royally with him. Not only by first breaking his trust, but by also then outing him in front of Kate. I never wanted to be a home-wrecker! Anyway, rather surprisingly, he actually came over and congratulated me on being right all along! He also told me that he and Kate were getting a divorce. I obviously said that I was sorry to hear his news (inwardly not!) ... but I also wondered whether he fancied going out for a drink. I wanted a chance to say sorry to him, as I knew that was totally my fault that he got a bloody nose.... And to my absolute shock, he said yes! He and Kate had been having problems for years. It wasn't just the hours. She just didn't trust him anymore. As I said before, her loss was definitely my gain. One drink turned into dinner, a nightcap, and then breakfast…. And then last week he moved in with me. Well, I have never been very patient! I love it… He now even manages to get his boxers in the wash basket, and it's great having a live-in soundboard… Over a lovely steak, we had even discussed the Gilling case… Who says romance is dead? I was trying to piece it all together. I had her phone examined, just in the interest of completeness. The tech guys had uncovered that it had a spy software installed, the type that covert ops used… Anyway, there was no paperwork to suggest that it had been done officially, so I had suspected John. He had spent time on attachment doings secret squirrel stuff, and I was going to flag his breach of RIPA, up to The Professional Standards Department.… "What are you going to do that for? You've got what you wanted. You were right! Maybe he was trying to catch her out?... It's not like you've ever done anything that wasn't quite above board is it?"

Of course, I knew exactly where he was going with this...

"... I think he and Shelley have been through enough don't you...?"

I wrestled with it, and I concluded that he might be right, not that I'll ever tell him that. So, for once I am letting sleeping dogs lie... After all, John let me off, so now I have returned the favour...

John

Immediately afterwards, I was put on compassionate leave. I had wanted to be there for Shelley and the girls, but to be honest, that wasn't the only reason, as to why I had been so grateful to HR for sorting it. I knew exactly how this all looked. I would be the talk of the Station yet again... I knew that they would be asking how could I not have known! I still can't work it out either. I have spent most of my life looking out for the enemy, it's why I won't sit in a bloody coffee shop window...

I could not believe that our lives, yet again had been turned upside down... and the only person that I could really see as responsible for that was Josephine. That bloody woman had torn my family apart and I couldn't say a negative word about her, as Shelley was completely broken at her loss. They say that grief is the love that has no place to go... Shelley had been hit with a double whammy and she had lost both of her mums at the exact same time. I know that she is trying to be strong for the girls, but at night when she thinks that we are all sleeping, I hear her sobs.

The press has hounded us… They came to the house; they blocked the road. It was chaos out there…… One of them ran the headline… SAINT OR SINNER? – YOU DECIDE! They had obviously slated the CPS, and the Judge for not having locked Josephine up the first time, but then they also ran a supplementary story, detailing her victim's pasts and their paedophilic tendencies. The public's opinion poll put her at 88% saint, although that was in 'The Daily Star!'

What I still don't understand, is why do this to Shelley, to your family? Why confess at all? What did it achieve, and why kill again? What had Wilkinson ever done to her? I had so many questions and no bloody answers!

There had been a time that all I had cared about was the truth, but that had changed a while back when I had made the decision to put my family first. It haunts me because maybe if I hadn't, this would never have happened.

Shelley

When the uniformed officers turned up at the house to tell me of my mother's death, I thought there had been some mistake. They had informed me that when she was checked on in the cell, she was already dead and no amount of CPR would have brought her back. I just couldn't work it out. Why was she even there? All they said was that she had been arrested. They wouldn't give me any further information. I was told that I would have to wait until the investigation was complete, and only then would they answer my questions. I did ask John to ask around for me, but he said that he couldn't. He was too embarrassed, as once again he would be the talk of the Nick. I quizzed him as to whether that was why Rachel had called him, but he swore blind that it was unconnected, and that he didn't know a thing.

Anyway, I didn't have to wait that long, as the next day there was a letter addressed to me on the mat. The postmark was from the previous day and as soon as I saw it, there was no questioning about it. It was definitely my biological mother's distinctive handwriting. I opened it hurriedly, and in it, she explained to me that she loved me more than anything and she had asked for my forgiveness. I don't think even she knew just how close she was to dying, but she did disclose that the cancer was terminal and because of this, she felt that she had had no choice. She had to right a number of wrongs. I think that was the main purpose of her letter. It was to make sure that I understood why she had done the things that she did. She did not want her crimes to taint my perception or memory of her. She didn't want to be judged by her past, only on her present. She had described how precious those last few months in France had been. She also hadn't wanted those memories spoilt by her becoming a burden, and me knowing that she was actually dying. She expressed the guilt that she still had over the death of Joseph, and for having sent not only me, but also Kelly Frost to prison. She highlighted that only recently due to our relationship, had she realised how important it was that she set the record straight. She had to give Kelly back her freedom... She said that she never wanted to leave me. And that she was hoping that she wouldn't actually be fit enough to serve any prison time and that maybe, we would still have those precious final days together...

However, when I discovered that she had killed again, and on the very day she had died, it had made absolutely no sense. I read that letter over and over, just in case I had missed something crucial, but there was no explanation …. Anyway, I didn't have to wait long to get my answer…. Once they had done the post mortem and cleared themselves from any wrongdoing in relation to her death, they released her body... and we were able to have the funeral. This funeral, I knew would be completely different from the one that we had had for my adoptive mother.

With Mum's funeral (Patty), the church was packed. My dad looked so smart in his black suit as he delivered the most heartfelt eulogy. He had put into words what everyone already knew. My mum was selfless. From the moment that he had met her, he had known that she was the one; and when they adopted me, their perfect lives were made just that bit better, by having a child to nurture and grow… He had said that I was the making of her, and her of me… He did briefly mention her fight with cancer but he kept the details of her struggle private; obviously in line with her final wishes. The wake afterwards was such a celebration of her life… Everyone had shared such wonderful and precious memories…

My biological mother's funeral was a different matter altogether. It was much more low key. She had left strict instructions that it was not to be in a church, so we went to the local crematorium... She had also requested that the song 'Toy Soldiers' by Martika be played at the service. I Googled it to find out its meaning, and I was a little surprised, that it had actually been written to highlight the dangers of drug use. I doubted that she had chosen it for that reason. Having read the lyrics, it did appear to be about a lost childhood and maybe that was why... Mum it seemed was never very good with songs... I remember being stood in the kitchen in France with her, and listening to 'Radio NOSTALGIE', and at the top of her voice, she sings... "I believe in Milko's... Where you from you sexy thing...." I turned to her and laughed, as ever since she had heard this in the 1970's, she had thought that these were the lyrics to Hot Chocolate's well-known hit. She had been belting them out for over 4 decades! How I had loved getting to know her!

Anyway, on that early December morning, I had only really expected that John, Dad, and I would be in attendance. I didn't want the girls to come, as I felt they were too young, and thankfully, at the time of the service, they were in school anyway. When I stood up at the front to say a few words, I looked out and I saw Jeanette (our neighbour), Imogen (Mum's old boss at the library), the newly promoted DI Rachel Cooper, and a few others at the back. One was a lady that I didn't immediately recognise. She appeared to be in her late 40's. A journalist perhaps? We had been promised that they would not attend, as it was a private service… but you couldn't trust them…

There I stood, next to her coffin and I started to speak about my mum… I had written something down, and I was going to explain how when I was growing up, I had always felt anxious and like something was missing, and I had never realised that the 'something' was my mum. I was going to share that by knowing her, I had gotten to know myself…. but then at the last minute, I decided not to read it. Instead, I began by explaining just how tragic my mother's life had been. I wanted people to know the other side of her story. What had shaped her as a person…. and not just what they had read about her in the papers. My mother, I felt, did right, by unfortunately doing wrong (I knew that this was not an opinion that John shared with me, however!) I highlighted the premature death of her father and that her childhood had been brutally cut short… (If this woman, or the other unknown attendees were from the press, I wanted them to report the fact that Mum had been a victim too.) Yes, her way of dealing with things was a little unorthodox, and people may judge her for the lives that she took, but for me, I only saw all of the lives that she had saved… and that had started with mine… I explained that her act of giving me up for adoption, was what had saved me, and that she had also saved my mum and dad from a lifetime of heartache. She gave them the gift of parenthood…. "My mum, in a way, also saved every one of those innocent victims... Their bogey man was forever gone; she had allowed them to sleep peacefully once again, and like them Mum, maybe you can too…. Sleep well. I love you…" I hadn't expected quite such an audience, but I felt pleased with what I had said. It captured how I felt and that was really all that mattered…

After the service, one of the unknown men who were stood at the back of the room came over to see me. He looked to be in his 50's, and he immediately hugged me and told me that he was sorry for my loss. He said that he had admired my mother.
"Sorry, who are you? How did you know Mum?"
"I didn't; I read about her in the papers, but what she did for me was amazing…"

I didn't initially understand what she had done for him, if he hadn't personally known her, but then he told me that he had been one of Geraint Pike's victims….

"She saved me, like you said."

He didn't say much more after that. I think he was embarrassed, however, I thanked him for coming, and I told him about the wake, but he said that he had to get back.

Then the lady that I couldn't place, also came up to speak to me. I had seen her having a friendly-looking chat with DI Cooper, so I amended my assumption of who she was, from Journalist to Police Officer…

"Sorry, do you mind if I have a word?"
"No, not at all. Thank you for coming. Do you work with DI Cooper?"

"Um, no, no I don't"

"I think I recognise you, but I'm sorry, I'm just not sure where from… I thought maybe police as I saw that you were talking to Rachel … You are not from the press, are you?" I say this immediately bristled…

"Oh, no, no definitely not! Rachel; she headed up the murder investigation into my partner's death."

"Oh…" I say a little surprised…

"I'm so sorry for your loss…"

"Don't be, I'm not… My partner, he was Gary Wilkinson…"

The penny drops, and I realise it was her partner that my mother killed…

"Oh my god! I'm so sorry… you are Jodie, Jodie Frost. I saw your picture in the paper…"

"Yes, that's right, but don't be sorry, your mum is a hero. She saved me not once, but twice, and what she did before she died, it has meant that my mum is being released next week from prison!"

It wasn't the response that I was expecting, as she had stood there gushing about how wonderful she thought my mum was... In fact, I had initially started to panic, thinking that she had come to have a go at me... Anyway, as I didn't understand what she meant about Mum saving her. I asked her the question... She in response started to roll up her sleeve, and then she showed me the numerous scars that she had on her arm, which were obviously from cigarette burns...

"I can't show you anything else, but my body is covered in all of the little reminders of what he did to me. The numerous punishments that he felt I had deserved..."

I think my face must have given away the fact that I couldn't understand why she would stay with clearly such a monster... As she then followed this up with...

"I was just too scared to leave him..."
"Oh, now I understand... So, my mum, in killing him, saved you?"

She then asked whether I would go outside with her... "to get some fresh air." I agreed to this as there was no one else waiting to give me their condolences... I followed her outside and through the large crematorium doors, and into the crisp winter sunshine... Once we were out of earshot of anyone else, she leant in and whispered into my ear...

"I can tell you this because you appear to see the grey, as well as all the shades in between..." I was a little confused by this ... but as she carried on, it all started to become clear...

"I could tell by what you said in your eulogy. You think that your mother is a hero too… I came here today because I need you to know what happened. I couldn't bear it, if by not knowing the truth, you would think badly of her…."

She inhaled deeply, and I felt the rush of her breath by my earlobe…and then she said…

"It wasn't her that killed him, it was me…"

As soon as she had said it, she stepped back and looked directly into my eyes, I think trying to judge my reaction… She then continued on with her story…

"He had been angry at me for spending money. He had gone to hit me again, and I don't know why, but something snapped, and I instinctively picked up the knife and that was it…. Before I knew it… I had stabbed him… Your mum, she just took the blame."

At that very moment, the few remaining pieces of the puzzle finally fitted together. My mother didn't have a thirst for killing, as some of the papers had alleged. My mum was just trying to do the right thing. We were stood outside in the cold for ages, but I felt warm as she described that day. She even explained why my mother had gone there in the first place. Jodie had taken a massive risk in telling me, but I saw no point in reporting her. After all, what would it achieve? It wouldn't change anyone's opinion of Mum, she was still a killer, and whether she was held accountable for 6 or the 7 victims, it was neither here nor there. All that would happen was that another daughter would lose her mother, and the cycle would begin all over again. It had been my mother's final wish and I would respect that. I promised her that I wouldn't tell a soul, not even John.

Later on, after the service, we all went to the local pub. It was the one that she used to go to with her dad, when she was a little girl, and it seemed the most fitting of send-offs. Jeanette came over to John and I… "Those were lovely words, Shelley…" She said, whilst giving me a hug… "No matter what she did. She will always be your mum…"

"Thanks, Jeanette. I know…. Actually, I'm glad you came, as I was wondering… Um, you see my compensation came through. We have enough to buy the Gite… Is it still for sale?"

"Um… Actually, that is the other reason as to why I came over to speak to you… I'm sorry, but it's already been sold." As she says this my face evidently drops. I had decided that after all of this, I just wanted to go back to a different life, one which was simpler and one where the only memories we had were happy. John was in agreement, and even Dad said he would come. Without Mum, he really had no reason to stay…

"Anyway, I just wanted to give you these..." As she said this, she puts the Gite keys into my hand.

"I don't understand... I thought you said it was already sold?"

"It is... Josephine bought it for you before she died. She gave strict instructions that I give you the keys once it had all gone through.... She wanted you to be able to go back there.... I think she knew that you would need somewhere to escape to..." Tears immediately begin to stream down my face...

"Oh my God, John! Did you hear what Jeanette said? Mum bought us the Gite! We can go back..."

"I did..." He says... I think a little speechless himself.... I can't believe how emotional I had become... I had kept myself together for most of the day, but now I was sobbing. I was thinking of all of the fun that Mum and I had had picking those bloody plums, and her larking about in the pool with the girls... Memories I thought I would have to work hard at remembering, but she had made sure that I would never forget.... John gave me

a hug, and as I sobbed over his shoulder, I saw that even DI Cooper had come to the wake. She was with Stu. They were now an item... I immediately tense up on seeing her. I step back from John as they make their way over to us. As I dry my eyes, Stu says to me.
"Sorry for your loss, Shelley. I didn't make it in time for the service, I got tucked up at work. You know how it is..."
"It's ok, I didn't really expect either of you to come... To be honest, I thought it would be just us family..." Rachel then speaks...
"Yes, I saw that you were talking to Jodie Frost. It seemed strange that she came?" Stu grabs Rachel's hand as if to stop her... Rachel looks over at him a little sheepish but then continues, although this time she seems nervous. She was rooting around in her handbag for something.
"Um... Yes, sorry... I am so sorry for your loss, Shelley. It must be hard..."

"Well, yes, it's not been easy…" And it really hadn't been… In such a short time, I had lost two of the most important people in my life. I knew that my adoptive mother was at peace, but Josephine? Her life had just been so chaotic… Rachel continued…

"Look, umm, there were a few bits of your mum's that weren't returned to you after the investigation… I think they were misplaced… I found them and I thought you might like to have them back…"

"Oh, Ok, thank you…" At this, she hands me a beer mat with the words 'The Inn Public House' printed on it. A sketch of 'Garfield the Cat' on an old hymn sheet … and a postcard… On it I immediately see that on one side there is a picture of the Virgin Mary, and on the other the following words;

May the Passion of our Lord Jesus Christ, the intercession of the Blessed Virgin Mary, and of all the saints, whatever good you do and suffering you endure, heal your sins, help you to grow in holiness, and reward you with eternal life. Go in peace.

It was the strangest collection of items, and it could only have been fate that brought them together. Maybe this was a message, her way of telling me that she was OK. The beer mat was from the pub where she had left me as a baby, the hymn sheet with the penned Garfield, could only have been from Barnaby, and the postcard with the prayer said it all…. It was there in black and white. It was the confirmation that I needed. My mum was finally at peace.

THE END.

This is a work of fiction. Names, characters, businesses, places, events, locales, and incidents are either the products of the author's imagination or used in a fictitious manner. Any resemblance to actual persons, living or dead, or actual events is purely coincidental.

A note from the author...

Thank you so much for taking the time to read my book. I really appreciate your support.

If you liked what you read, or even if you didn't, please feel free to leave me some constructive feedback.

If you did enjoy this however, and want to read another book written by me...why not try **The Pilot's Wife**. *Available to download as an e-book on Kindle or as a paperback edition on Amazon.*

If you want to keep up to date with my latest projects, or you just want to know more about me, why not follow me on Amazon, or visit my website

www.kecullenwriter.co.uk

Printed in Great Britain
by Amazon